THE INEXPLICABLE UNHAPPINESS
OF RAMU HAJJAM

Taj Hassan lives in Delhi with his wife and son. *The Inexplicable Unhappiness of Ramu Hajjam* is his first novel. He can be contacted at tajhassan2001@gmail.com.

The Inexplicable Unhappiness of Ramu Hajjam

TAJ HASSAN

hachette
INDIA

First published in 2012 by Hachette India
(Registered name: Hachette Book Publishing India Pvt. Ltd)
An Hachette UK company
www.hachetteindia.com

SRD

ISBN 978-93-5195-197- 1

Hachette Book Publishing India Pvt. Ltd
4th/5th Floors, Corporate Centre,
Plot no. 94, Sector 44, Gurgaon 122003, India

Typeset in Cochin LT Std 10.5/13.5
by InoSoft Systems Noida

Printed and bound in India by
Manipal Technologies Limited, Manipal

FSC www.fsc.org
MIX
Paper from responsible sources
FSC™ C043100

To

Nuzhat and Sarmad

Prologue

The Kareh flowed throughout the year.

During the rains it swelled its banks and grew full-bodied; not even an elephant dared cross it then. But when the clouds receded it shrivelled to a thin trickle in a vast tract of sand, flowing sedately, pausing a moment, then pushing forward again. People believed its source was in an unknown valley high in the Vindhyas, though none was certain of this. They were all in agreement however that the Kareh was a life-line thrown down by the gods for the villages of Bhagatpur and, down-river, for Tesri.

People from both villages drank the waters of the same river. Life in both villages revolved around it. None can remember exactly when the situation changed. But change it did, in an insidious and relentless fashion, after a fight broke out between the villages. People began to dread going to the riverbank for fear of ending up dead, hacked to bits.

And so the fight continued, polarizing everybody.

You were either on this side or that.

The Kareh watched silently as the tension between the villages grew. Through the ages, it had witnessed waves of people arrive, settle on its banks, fight each other and then vanish without trace, without ever being able to fathom what they were doing.

As always, the river was indifferent.

1.

It was a regular day in Tesri, but then Tesri rarely had one that was not.

Ramu Hajjam woke early, sweating profusely though it was the month of March and the mornings still had a slight nip to them. Normally he rose with the first call of a rooster somewhere in the village, followed by the call of the muezzin from the mosque without a minaret. But that night he had dreamt of his father Kalu Hajjam, coughing and spitting blood that had spread slowly, soaking first the checkered hand-towel that he always carried on his shoulder and then seeping through the fabric of his shirt. Ramu was troubled by this vision and had paced restlessly about his room. His father's life came back vividly to his mind.

Back then, besides shaving and trimming hair, it was customary for the men of his caste – the barber caste – to double as news-messengers and to extend invitations to weddings, births and funerals on behalf of landholders to other households in nearby villages. Following tradition, Ramu's father Kalu Hajjam had initiated his son early into the family profession. Ramu accompanied his father as he trekked from village to village. He was happy to do this because the invitees rewarded his father for the tidings with gifts of grain and cloth and, sometimes, fed them sumptuously besides.

Of all these moments, Ramu Hajjam had fond memories.

But then one day, when he was still a young boy, his father had developed a rasping cough. A few days later he had begun to run a high fever and finally he threw up blood. It was all downhill after that. One day, when he was trying to lift himself up from his charpoy, his father keeled over, and never stood up again.

Immediately after the customary thirteen-day mourning period Ramu's mother Kalavati Devi made a bonfire of all his father's belongings, even tossing his father's cot into the flames. She wanted to make sure that the tuberculosis germs that had killed her husband would not infect the other members of her family.

When he woke that morning Ramu Hajjam felt an inexplicable sadness because in his dream he saw his father in agony, futilely trying to tell him something but not being able to and crumpling to the floor before he could finish. By the time the muezzin finished his call, Ramu had left the room, leaving his wife Phulmani sound asleep. It was still dark and he could not stop thinking about the dream and the grief-lined face of his father.

He came out of his room to the corner of the veranda where his mother and his adolescent son Pawan slept. The corner at the far end functioned as a kitchen during the winter and the rains. That day, to his surprise, he found his mother sitting up in her bed, lost deep in thought, the wrinkles on her face accentuated by the fading light of a kerosene lantern.

He had the strange feeling that his mother had seen the same dream as he, but something stopped him from asking her about it.

He dressed slowly, all the while trying to suppress the overwhelming sadness that engulfed him, but he could not shake off the dream and his dead father's unsuccessful attempts to tell him something.

As he was leaving for Bhagatpur, to his barber-shop in the haat there, his mother Kalavati fixed him with a strange look. 'Be careful of the March wind. It is very dangerous and causes serious illnesses,' she said.

Now he was convinced that his mother had had the same dream.

When he reached the haat, there was nobody around except for Israfil Mian and Chhotu, his errand-boy, who was trying to stoke the fire in the hearth to set the kettle on it. Ramu Hajjam picked up his chair and the small plastic bag that contained the tools of his trade – Israfil Mian's teashop was the only safe place in the haat and many of the smaller vendors used to leave their belongings there.

Israfil Mian looked at him and said, 'Ramu bhai, you are looking unwell. What has happened to you?'

Ramu smiled vaguely as he really could not put a finger on it himself.

⌘

Ramu Hajjam set up shop under the neem tree. His shop comprised a rickety chair and a mirror that hung from a nail embedded in the tree. Every day he sat on the ground or in the chair, waiting for customers. They came – known faces from his own village and Bhagatpur or strangers passing through from sundry neighbouring villages – in good numbers only on Sunday. On other days he had just the odd customer and whiled away his time shooting the breeze with Akbar Mian, whose cycle-repair shop was next to his.

It was particularly windy and dusty that day. Brittle yellow leaves floated down from the trees. On such days it was his practice to tie a plastic sheet just above the chair to shelter his customers from the falling leaves and sprigs. But, that morning, he felt unaccountably lazy and thought he would tie the sheet if a customer happened along. After chatting with Akbar Mian for a while he forgot the dream he had seen last night and fell into a light doze.

There was no sign of any customer till noon and he was planning to close shop early when, suddenly, Subedar Singh parked his bicycle near Akbar Mian's stall and came and sat down heavily on the chair. 'I have come for a shave,' he announced.

Ramu Hajjam knew Subedar Singh. He was an arrogant and haughty man from Bhagatpur. He put a squeeze of shaving cream on Subedar Singh's cheeks and expertly worked up a lather with the help of his worn-out brush. Then he sharpened his shaving blade on a leather strop and began working Subedar Singh's cheeks. At that precise moment, as luck would have it, a squirrel on the tree above caused a dried sprig to fall. It fell straight on Ramu's hand, and his hand jerked, inflicting a small cut on Subedar Singh's right cheek.

Ramu Hajjam froze.

The next moment, he was on the ground. Subedar Singh was sitting on his chest, punching him hard, hurling abuses at him. 'You filthy bastard! How dare you?' he screamed.

All the people sitting in the teashop ran to the scene and gathered about the neem tree. They watched silently, from a safe distance.

Subedar Singh was finished with Ramu only when he realized that a corner of his dhoti had caught in the chair and any further attempts to move would be at the cost of a snag. He got up, kicked Ramu one last time, picked up his bicycle and pedalled away.

Ramu Hajjam had lost consciousness.

When Subedar Singh was no longer in sight, the people who had gathered around mustered the courage to sprinkle water on Ramu's face. Somebody got a charpoy from the teashop. They laid him down gently on it and then four people picked it up and left for Tesri.

Holding the charpoy aloft, as if he were already dead.

⌘

Ramu Hajjam had no recollection of being carried home. He was unaware that his wife, crying and beating her chest, had run up to the outskirts of the village to receive him. He was unaware that the four persons carrying the charpoy had not stopped on the way and lowered the bed only when they reached the courtyard of his house. He was unaware that, on hearing of the incident, almost the entire village had turned out to see him – some in sympathy, some to gawk. He was unaware that his seventeen-year-old son was now by his side, crying soundlessly.

After a while, though, he registered voices in the distance. Then the voices seemed to grow closer. He heard someone say, 'Give way for air.' When he opened his eyes he saw Murli Compounder putting a stethoscope to his chest. Ramu's eyes searched about frantically trying to locate his wife in the crowd until he realized that she too was right there, beside him, holding his hand. She had tears in her eyes.

'He has regained consciousness!' someone shouted the obvious.

After examining him, Murli Compounder declared: 'There are no apparent problems, but he needs to rest to recover from the shock.'

The people were relieved. They looked at Murli Compounder with the admiration and respect accorded to a hero.

2.

Achal Singh Mukhia sat on a reclining chair in the large open courtyard of his house in the Choudhary Tola section of Bhagatpur village. There were several charpoys laid out in neat rows before him on which men of different ages lay or sat, chatting.

Dressed in pristine white, a flowing, cotton-white beard on his fair flushed face, Achal Singh Mukhia looked every bit the venerable Bhishma Pitamah from the Mahabharata.

But everyone in the village knew that his temperament was quite unlike Bhishma Pitamah's; he was more of a Duryodhan.

Mukhia had no sons. His three daughters had been married long ago. They lived with their husbands far from Bhagatpur and rarely visited their father. Mukhia's nephew Ashok Singh looked after Mukhia's property.

Achal Singh had been the mukhia of the village for so many years that the people could no longer remember whether he had been elected to the post or nominated to it. Mukhia – village headman – had become his second name. Achal Singh cherished this name.

The main village under his jurisdiction, Bhagatpur, was divided into three segments. The largest segment, Choudhary Tola, comprised a hundred and fifty houses of landowning, mainly uppercaste folk, a few of whom were big landlords like Achal Singh Mukhia but the majority of whom were petty and impoverished farmers.

To the north of Choudhary Tola lay Teli Tola, a smaller settlement of thirty houses of Telis – traders and businessmen – some of whom ran the oil-press mill after which the settlement was named.

Fifty metres down from Teli Tola was Dhobi Tola, made up of fifteen hutments of dhobis and sundry lowcastes who did the menial work for the people of Choudhary Tola.

Most of the villagers in Bhagatpur lived a fairly content life because they had not seen much of the world outside. Their lives were limited to the Kareh river, to the fields on which they worked, and to their homesteads – extending, at most, to Achal Singh Mukhia's large courtyard where they relaxed and discussed threadbare every issue within the purview of their knowledge.

Some of the poorer farmers had migrated to cities far and wide to earn their livelihood because the produce from their field was too meagre to feed them through the year. They worked as construction labourers, as taxi drivers, as waiters in hotels. When they came back to the village they too gathered on the Mukhia's veranda.

More so of late, as fear had made them flock together.

The news from across the river was that the men of their caste – small and big landholders, even poor peasant farmers – were being chased away by a group that called itself the Maoists.

The Maoists had taken control of the area across the river. They had the support of people from the lower and backward castes – people, who till a few months ago, did not even have the gumption to sit before the high-castes without their permission, or even look them in the eye.

So, these days especially, the villagers of Bhagatpur gathered in the mukhia's veranda after finishing their work in the fields, to align their thoughts with the suggestions and conjectures of Achal Singh Mukhia's high-born mind.

To the mukhia's dissatisfaction, however, there were a handful of people in the village who had resisted all attempts to come under his hegemony. Pratap Singh and his extended family were one such example.

Many years ago, Pratap Singh had been Achal Singh's arch rival in the village but he had been forced out after a bloody feud with him. So Pratap Singh had settled a little further away, in Dumri Chowk, three miles from Bhagatpur, where the village mud road met the cemented state highway. Here, four times a day, an overloaded bus of indeterminate colour halted for a few minutes and carried the villagers twenty miles away to Puraini Railway Station, from where the passengers then made their way to the bigger cities in search of jobs. Pratap Singh ran a teashop near the bus-stand. Over the years, a few other shops had sprung up near his stall making the spot quite popular, at least during the daytime when the buses plied.

Positioned in his teashop, Pratap Singh worked assiduously to oppose the mukhia's every act by talking against him to every customer who walked in; turning the neutral against him, and forging alliances with his enemies.

⌘

Tesri, Ramu Hajjam's village, was about a mile away from Bhagatpur, on the way to the Dumri bus-stand, and a mile further still, from the main mud road. It was a poor, nondescript village. Here lived the barbers, cobblers, washermen, earth-diggers, sweepers and scavengers – all those dregs of society born into the most menial work-castes since the world began. They accepted the squalour of their lives as their destiny, hoping that their next life would bring better luck.

It was said that, till not so long ago, and if the big landlords of Bhagatpur so desired, when a newly-wed bride arrived in the village she would have to spend her suhaag raat, her first night of married life, with one of them. As a direct corollary to this, it was also said that if anyone in Tesri had any guts at all it was only because he had the blood of the landlords of Bhagatpur running in his veins.

When a passing Maulvi pitched up tent in Tesri and began handing out talismans to the needy and the sick, no one seemed to notice. Nor were they sure when, for that matter, a thatched-roof mosque came up in the village. The people of Tesri named the area around the mosque Kunjra Toli as the lowcaste Muslims who lived there earned their livelihood from growing and selling vegetables.

Tesri had a large clear patch of ground at its centre, at the focus point of which grew a huge banyan tree, probably as old as the village itself. The villagers had fashioned a mud platform around the trunk, on which they sat and chatted in their spare time, of which they had plenty. All the narrow alleys in the village led here. In the evenings, idle old men and unemployed youth whiled away their time playing cards and listening to the crackling of Jamuna Das's radio.

Most of the villagers who lived in Tesri earned their livelihood from the bazaar in Bhagatpur, which was where the dirt-track from the village merged with the main mud road. It was the only source of entertainment for the people of Bhagatpur and its surrounding villages. But the haat came alive only on Sundays, when all the villagers would walk down to the makeshift market to buy their weekly provisions, or just to loaf about, meeting acquaintances and having fun.

Only a handful of vendors put up their stalls every day in the vain hope of attracting a stray customer. On such days a desolate wind blew over the bazaar ground as a straggle of people sat themselves down on the wooden benches of Israfil Mian's teashop, sipping tea and gossiping. Housed in a room with a tiled roof, it was the only permanent structure on that vast, dusty ground, and the centre of gossip for the whole area.

This, then, was Tesri in the year 1991.

3.

Till a year ago, Jamuna Das had been a bonded labourer on Achal Singh Mukhia's farm. When his son grew up, he had the boy replace him at his job, and opened a small grocery store in Tesri. He wanted to devote his time to the betterment of his village. Tesri had no separate post for a village head as it came under the panchayat of Bhagatpur of which Achal Singh was the mukhia, but, for all practical purposes, for the villagers of Tesri, Jamuna Das was the man they looked up to.

Jamuna Das's shop did well and soon he bought a second-hand radio. Every evening he sat under the banyan tree with his radio on. The men of the village would gather around to listen to the evening programme of folk music, bulletins on agriculture and the news. Nobody from the village was literate and the radio became their only window – and Jamuna Das their default authority – on the outside world.

Perhaps that was why people had accepted him as their village head.

That day only the leaves of the huge banyan tree rustled in the westerly wind. Everyone was a little subdued because of the incident at the bazaar.

Someone suggested, 'It is news time. Let us put the radio on.' Jamuna Das thought it would be a good way to dispel the gloom and turned it on.

The news-reader said: 'The government has announced special measures to prevent atrocities on the downtrodden sections of society...'

'We don't want to listen to these platitudes! We should decide what to do about today's incident!' one of the young men protested.

Everyone looked uneasily at the boy. The subject was on each one's mind but none spoke of it. Jamuna Das recognized the lad. He worked as a mason in Kolkata and had come back to the village for the harvest. The young boys who worked in the big cities always came back to the village with big revolutionary ideas. Jamuna Das sighed and switched off the radio.

'Some days ago Sundari Devi was molested just because her goat was grazing in the fields of Jagir Singh from Bhagatpur. We went to Achal Singh Mukhia but he ridiculed us and threw us out. Now Ramu Hajjam has been beaten up mercilessly. Are we going to the police? Or at least to Achal Singh Mukhia, our village head?' The boy was clearly agitated.

Nobody spoke for a long time. A bird sitting on a branch of the banyan tree hooted, probably confusing the moonlit night for the break of dawn. Eventually, someone said, 'He is right. We should go to meet Achal Singh Mukhia tomorrow. And if he does not respond, we will go to the police.'

At that precise moment they saw Subedar Singh cycling down towards them. He stopped, stood his bicycle on its stand, and approached them menacingly. Then he started shouting: 'You bastards! I know you are conspiring against me. I will teach you all a lesson!'

He pulled out a vermilion-stained lance – used to unfurl Lord Hanuman's flag – that was embedded by the root of the banyan tree, put it across his thigh and snapped it into two. Everyone fled the scene except Jamuna Das, terrified though he was that he might be beaten up. But Subedar Singh didn't do anything to him. He hurled the broken pieces of the lance to the ground, mounted his bicycle and pedalled away.

The next day no one in the village said a word about going to Achal Singh Mukhia or to the police.

⌘

When Murli Compounder – checking-up on him the following day – put his stethoscope to his chest, Ramu Hajjam's eyes glazed over a second time and he slipped into a subconscious state. In his trance, Ramu dreamt of a saint with a halo around his head and a face that radiated a serene peace. The saint sat on a high pedestal adorned with beautiful carvings. Before him stood a king with his head bowed.

The saint asked the king, 'Why have you come here, Your Majesty?'

And the king said, 'I had a dream early this morning. When I told my state purohit about it, he said that the dream foretold evil. He said that I would need to make sacrifices to avert a calamity. I want to know the meaning of my dream.'

And the saint said, 'Tell me about your dream, Your Majesty.'

And the king said: 'I saw a vast field, the centre of which was fertile and green, abloom with sweet-smelling flowers and exotic trees, but the area around the periphery of the field was barren. Surprisingly, the citizenry all lived on the periphery and were scared to go to the central area. The dream has upset me. Tell me, what could it mean?'

And the saint said that the dream implied that in the days to come, kings would become unrighteous and wilful. They would not follow rules and would show no mercy. They would keep around them people who were unrighteous and merciless like themselves. They would harass the poor for no reason and tax them oppressively. Unable to pay the taxes or survive the extortionist ways of the king and his loyalists, the poor people would flee to the borders of the kingdom.

And the king asked, 'When will this happen?'

And the saint said, 'Not in your reign, Your Majesty. You rule with righteousness. This will come to pass in the distant future.'

And Ramu Hajjam heard himself shouting, 'It has come! Look at me, look at my condition! That time has *come*!'

But then he saw that both the king and the saint were no longer in his dream. He tried to run after them but total darkness engulfed him and he woke drenched in sweat, only to find his wife, Phulmani, weeping by his bedside. Murli Compounder was saying something, but he could not hear what it was because he was still lost in the fog of his dream.

Ramu Hajjam realized that day that he dreamt strange dreams whenever he was traumatized. And his dreams bore meanings that he could not share with anyone.

4.

Murli Compounder was the nearest thing they had to a doctor in Tesri. He was often seen cycling around the village with a plastic bag that contained basic medicines, first-aid supplies, a rusty stethoscope and syringes and needles of assorted gauges. Over the years he had become so famous that people from neighbouring villages – even from Bhagatpur – came to consult him.

Many years ago, when Murli was very young, probably about sixteen or seventeen, he realized that he had no real future in Tesri. His father owned an oil-press mill from which oil was squeezed from mustard by a wooden grinder hitched to a pair of buffaloes that walked around the grinder in unending circles. Murli had many siblings – four brothers and three sisters. His father was somewhat better off than the other people of the village, so Murli had attended school for a bit. But he had to drop out after class five and then he had nothing to do.

His father's mill did not have too many customers in the village, so Murli started working as a cattle-grazer for the landholders of Bhagatpur. One day, he decided to run away to Kolkata – the big city he had heard of, where so many young boys from the village had gone to find work and earn a livelihood.

He confided his plans to his mother who was against his decision. 'You are very young and have two older brothers. If someone from this family has to go it will be your eldest brother.'

But he was adamant. He said, 'I will go. And you will have to manage Baba after I leave because there's no way that I'm going to tell him this.'

So choosing the rainiest day of the monsoon season because he knew that his father would not be able to chase him down in the rain and bring him back, Murli ran away.

He walked all the way to the bus-stand and caught a bus to Puraini Railway Station. From there he took a train to Kolkata and fell asleep, just as he was, drenched and exhausted, as soon as he sat down on the wooden berth.

He woke up to utter commotion. The train stood in a lonely spot amidst the flooded fields that stretched to the horizon on either side of the tracks. He heard someone say, 'The train will go no further. The bridge across the river has been washed away in the flood.' He started to worry. Where would he go? He had only fifteen rupees in his pocket, which his mother had given him on the assurance that he would write to her after reaching Kolkata.

The rain had stopped and people were clambering out of the bogie to find out the situation for themselves. A few passengers were still hopeful that the train would start and remained seated inside the carriage. Murli was deeply worried but going back to the village was out of the question as he would have to face his father's wrath. He was interested only in going to Kolkata to earn his livelihood, and he prayed that the train would start soon.

After a couple of hours a passenger came back in and announced, 'The train is not going to go any further. Ismailpur, the nearest railway station, is two miles behind. Let us walk down there. At least we will have shelter and something to eat.' Hearing him, the few passengers who remained inside the compartment got up to leave. All the passengers from his carriage left one by one.

Murli was all alone. He was scared and close to tears. The sun was out now and the greenery on both sides of the track presented a beautiful sight. Murli got off the train but decided not to go back to the last station. He could see a village in the distance, to the right of the railway track, and Murli started walking towards it. He walked on the muddy foot-track for more than two hours. It was getting dark when he reached the village.

Approaching the outskirts of the village he saw a two-storeyed building and decided that he would request the owner of the house to give him food and shelter, at least till the tracks and bridge were repaired. Walking up to the building he saw a board with a large red plus sign and 'Arogyadham, Dhanwar' written in bold letters, in Hindi, nailed to the wall. He understood that it was a hospital. He sat on the cement bench near the main gate of the building. He remained seated there for a long time but could not summon the courage to knock on the door.

Finally, a middle-aged man wearing a white kurta and dhoti came outside. Seeing Murli he asked, 'Who are you? Are you ill?' Murli told him about his journey and how he had come to be there, and then asked for shelter and food.

Murli was to learn subsequently that the man's name was Sundaram. He ran a non-government organization in that remote rural area, of which this hospital was part.

He took Murli inside, offered him food and a bed for the night, and told him to stay as long as he wished. Instead of just waiting there for the bridge to be repaired, Murli started to make himself useful from the very next day. In a few days, he forgot that he had ever wanted to go to Kolkata.

He wrote a letter to his mother about himself, and about the work he was doing. He told his mother that she should not worry about him because he was very happy in the new place, and that he would write to her regularly. He did not write his address, fearing that his father would come to see him or send someone to bring him back, because he knew that his village was not very far from Dhanwar.

He began work as a pharmacist's assistant and within a few months became an expert pharmacist himself. Within a year he could handle patients without any help from Sundaram. He could prescribe medicines for common ailments and even became adept at administering injections.

Murli stayed on in Dhanwar for more than five years. During that time he trained himself to become a competent pharmacist, albeit without a recognized degree. He also learnt how to run a non-government organization. He grew close to Sundaram, who took him along on field projects and on his visits to the district authorities. Working with Sundaram Murli grew into a hard-working and disciplined man.

After five years with Sundaram at Arogyadham, he decided to return to his village. He told Sundaram, 'I want to set up a medical practice in my own village where there is no doctor, not even a trained compounder, and people have to go to a far-off town when they are ill. Anyway, my village is only four hours from here. I will keep coming back to meet you.'

When he was leaving, Sundaram gifted him a bag containing the basic equipment a medical practitioner would need. It contained a stethoscope, syringes, a device for measuring blood pressure, and some medicines for common ailments.

He returned to Tesri in the month of August. The alternating spells of rain and strong sun had made the weather unbearably humid. Many people were falling sick during that time, suffering from an inexplicable fever that did not lessen its grip for a full seven days. Murli used the knowledge he had gained at

Arogyadham and the medicines Sundaram had given him to treat the affected villagers. Word spread about him. Very soon he became famous in all the near-by villages. That he did not have a genuine medical degree made no difference.

Besides practising medicine in the village, Murli tried his hand at all those things that Sundaram had done under the banner of his NGO. But, unlike Sundaram, he did not do it for charity. He ran a school on his premises and, after lessons were over, sent the schoolboys to graze his cattle. When poor villagers came to him asking for a loan he obliged them only if they pawned their cattle to him. As most of the villagers were never able to pay back the loan amount, Murli kept their cattle and, in the course of time, accumulated a large herd.

In no time Murli became Tesri's most influential and wealthy resident. After the banyan tree in the main chowk, his clinic became the local landmark. Outside it he hung a board with a plus sign and the words 'Dr Murli, R.M.P.' inscribed on it.

What the initials stood for, no one had a clue.

5.

Ramu Hajjam had grown very withdrawn after the incident. His silence was a cause of great concern for his wife as well as his mother. Whenever they asked him anything he would respond with a nod or a vague gesture. Initially, Phulmani thought he would return to normal in a day or two. But things did not improve even after four days; Ramu Hajjam seemed to shrink deeper and deeper into his shell. She was concerned not only about his silence, but also about the depleting provisions in her kitchen. Their life depended on his daily earnings and this prolonged sickness of the head of the family – their sole breadwinner – made her nervous. She believed Murli when he said that her husband had no disease. But she could not fathom the reason for his silence.

On the fifth day, Phulmani decided that no medicine would cure her husband. What was needed was a talisman. She knew where she could get one and she went to get it herself.

⌘

Phulmani waited outside the gate of the mosque in Kunjra Toli. It was time for the evening prayer. It was almost dark when the Maulvi came out of the mosque.

Phulmani recognized the Maulvi immediately, as she had seen him often, sitting under the banyan tree. He was an old man with a white beard and walked with his back held straight despite his age.

'Namaskar,' she said.

The Maulvi wasn't expecting a visitor at that time, least of all a woman. He looked at her in surprise and tried to place her.

'I am Ramu Hajjam's wife,' Phulmani said.

The Maulvi had heard of the incident at the haat and immediately guessed her reason for coming to him.

'How is your husband?' he asked.

'Otherwise all right, except he has not spoken for the last five days. I am worried. What has happened to him? I have come here to ask you for help.'

The Maulvi went inside his room, took a box of matches from his pocket and lit a lantern. Then he rummaged through some papers on his table. He found the book he needed, looked something up in its pages and scribbled a few words on a piece of paper.

He folded the paper many times over and put it in a small tin amulet tied to a thread. He handed this over to Phulmani. 'He will be all right. Just hang this talisman around his neck,' he said.

Tears rolled down her eyes. Phulmani thanked the Maulvi profusely and asked him to pray for her husband.

It was pitch dark when she reached home. Her mother-in-law, Kalavati, was waiting for her in the veranda looking shrunken and forlorn. The wrinkles on her face were accentuated by the dim light of the lantern. Ramu Hajjam was sitting on his bed, lost in his thoughts, and Pawan sat on the veranda beside Kalavati.

The abnormal silence in the house alarmed Phulmani. It was as if somebody had died.

'We were waiting for you. Where have you been?' Kalavati asked accusingly

'Just went outside to consult somebody.' She didn't want to divulge the details.

'I thought I would wait for you before cooking dinner. We are running out of provisions.' There was a deep melancholy in Kalavati's voice.

Phulmani was upset that the evening fire in the kitchen had not been lit. It was a bad omen. And if her husband remained the way he was they would soon die of hunger. Six days of his illness had brought them to the brink of starvation.

She wondered what she would do if her husband's condition did not improve. Jamuna Das would not give her provisions on loan from his shop. She would either have to work in the fields, or send Pawan to work in the barbershop. But the poor boy did not even know how to give a shave! She looked intently at each of them, one by one, and said, 'I will cook whatever we have. In the morning, we will see what is to be done.'

In the night, when everyone had fallen asleep, she went to her husband's bed and fastened the talisman around his neck. 'The Maulvi has given it,' she said when he awoke. 'He says you will soon be all right.'

Ramu Hajjam said nothing.

'If you remain this way we are going to die of hunger.'

He looked up at this. There was a certain resolve in his eyes. Maybe he had heard her talking to Kalavati and knew that there were not enough provisions in the house to sustain the family for even one more day.

'I will go to the haat tomorrow. You don't worry,' he said.

Phulmani heaved a sigh of relief. The Maulvi's talisman had worked its magic.

6.

Next morning, exactly a week after the incident, Ramu Hajjam got ready to return to the haat and open his shop. He was still quite reticent, as if words had become a scarce commodity for him. Phulmani was happy though, convinced that the daily routine of life would coax him out of his shell. She decided to send Pawan along with his father so that he too could start learning the family profession and take on the responsibility of the family in case the situation demanded.

Father and son started for the haat at ten in the morning. Ramu Hajjam was still unprepared for the prying questions of the villagers who spent most of their time sitting idle under the banyan tree. He didn't want to interact with anybody. Fortunately, there was nobody sitting under the tree as they passed by it.

The haat too was deserted when they arrived. It was a windy day with bright sunlight. Ramu Hajjam went straight to the teashop where he stored his chair and his tools.

'Namaskar,' he greeted Israfil Mian.

'Namaskar, Ramu Bhai. How are you?' Israfil Mian enquired.

'Fine, Israfil Mian. I have come to open my shop.'

A couple of bamboo charpoys were laid out in a straight line in front of the teashop. There was nobody in the shop at that time, except Israfil Mian and his odd-jobs boy. The sun was warm but not unbearable.

'Arrey, sit down, Ramu Bhai. Have a cup of tea,' Israfil Mian said.

Ramu Hajjam sat down on a cot and asked Pawan to collect the chair and tools and set up shop, but Israfil Mian intervened: 'He will also have a cup of tea.'

Israfil Mian's boy started working the stove, blowing air with a hand fan to get the fire going so that he could put on some tea for the three of them.

'You know, Ramu Bhai, what happened to you was very bad. But the incident is going to have far-reaching repercussions,' Israfil Mian said.

Ramu Hajjam felt that Israfil Mian was just trying to be sympathetic. He said, 'How? Landowners thrashing a poor man like me can have no far-reaching consequences.'

'Ramu Bhai, people come to this shop even from far-off villages. Everyone passing by this way stops for a cup of tea and a chat. I hear things,' Israfil Mian explained.

A stray dog sitting near the cot got up, stretched lazily, and trotted off behind the shop wagging its tail. A sudden gust of wind blew dust across the bazaar ground. The boy served them tea. Israfil Mian took a sip and continued: 'After the incident last Saturday, three men from across the river came to enquire about it. They said that they would decide the matter in their court. They were Maoists. They have complete control of the area across the Kareh.'

Ramu Hajjam had often heard his customers talk about these people. He had been told that across the Kareh, the Maoists had control of everything and that there was no government there. He had also been told that the Maoists were against all landowners and were forcing them off their land. He had not paid much attention to this talk as it didn't concern him. Now, for the first time, he started thinking seriously about what they had said. He was worried because he feared that any further escalation of the dispute would only bring him harm.

'We are poor people. We have nothing to do with the Maoists or the landlords. We were like this in the past and we will remain like this in the future,' Ramu Hajjam said, draining the last of his tea. 'Now let me go and put up the plastic sheet.'

⌘

It was a good day for Ramu Hajjam. Two customers came to his shop for a haircut. He felt happy – Phulmani would breathe a sigh of relief seeing some money at last.

7.

The next day being Sunday, Ramu and Pawan arrived early at the haat. It was Ramu Hajjam's second day at work after a week-long convalescence. He was still a little lost in his thoughts and spoke little. What Israfil Mian had told him the previous day, though, was still playing on his mind.

That day, the haat was bustling with people. The atmosphere was decidedly festive. Women clad in colourful saris, balancing babies on their hips, were busy purchasing various household articles. Children ran around enjoying colourful ice-lolly sticks. People from neighbouring villages were present in full strength hoping to buy and sell goats, cows and bullocks, besides articles of daily use. On Sundays, Ramu Hajjam would use the money he made to buy provisions for the week.

In the afternoon, when the crowd at the haat was at its peak, three strangers came to his shop.

The three men planted themselves in front of him boldly. 'Are you Ramu Hajjam?' one of them asked.

Ramu Hajjam tried to remember whether he had seen them before. 'Yes, I am. What do you want?' They looked no different from the other villagers.

'We want nothing. We have come from across the river. We want to know what happened to you last Saturday. What we heard was that it was a case of atrocity by the landowner class. We intervene in all such cases and ensure justice,' one of them said.

Ramu Hajjam was afraid. How could he fight against the landowners of Bhagatpur under whose protection and servitude his father and forefathers had lived, and under whose mercy he too was living? It was impossible, he thought, and decided to say nothing to these men, even if they beat him up and humiliated him in public. He looked at them worriedly and then realized they did not look like criminals to him. Their manner was normal, even polite.

'I don't have any complaint against anybody. I am happy the way I am,' Ramu Hajjam said firmly.

The three men stood there and gave Ramu Hajjam an assessing look. Pawan, standing behind his father, quietly observed everything.

'The time has come for you people to fight back. Otherwise the landowners will keep on harassing you, humiliating your daughters and sisters. Across the river, we have threatened them. They don't have the guts to do anything so openly to us,' the man said.

'Think it over. We do not live far from here. You can contact us in Mukhdoompur,' one of the other men said.

Abruptly, they turned and walked away.

A split second later, Ramu saw Pawan running after them. He too ran after his son, and heard him ask the men, 'How far is your village?'

'Just three miles from here,' one of them replied.

Ramu Hajjam could not believe his ears! Pawan was just seventeen. Seeing him follow the Maoists and ask them their address, sent a shiver down his spine. That's when it dawned on him that Israfil Mian had been right.

Last Saturday's incident was going to have far-reaching consequences.

8.

The passenger train lurched to a halt at Puraini Railway Station. Within moments, the otherwise sleepy platform came alive.

Tea vendors started soliciting customers at the top of their voices – 'Hot tea, hot milky tea!' – and poured the steaming chai into earthen cups from the kettle even before it was ordered. Beggars hobbled about making their rounds, moving from one stationary compartment to the next, stretching their palms plaintively in front of everyone, wheedling them to part with their hard-earned money. Even the stray dogs got up, stretched themselves and looked about with hopeful eyes.

Puraini station was in the middle of nowhere. The nearest village was a mile away. Because it was the only railway link for more than twenty villages, a small market had gradually established itself – teashops, a couple of provision stores, a newspaper stand and a few roadside hotels. Outside the railway station, was a bus-stop. It was busier than the railway station since most of the villages were linked by bus.

Lakhan Subedar got off the train and pulled out his luggage – a black tin trunk, marked 'Subedar Lakhan, 27 Infantry Division, 56 APO' in bold white paint, a roll of olive-green bedding and a plastic handbag. Twenty years in the army had taught him not to be dependent on anyone. After pulling out his luggage he looked around to see if someone had come from Bhagatpur to receive him. Not seeing anybody, he was about to set off alone when he spotted his nephew come running towards him. He was there with a friend. Both the boys greeted him and touched his feet.

'Sorry, we're late. We were having tea by the bus-stop and came running when we heard the whistle of the train,' his nephew said.

Lakhan Subedar allowed the boys to carry his luggage for him. In the course of his long army career he had travelled all over the country. Now he would only have to travel to the nearby town to collect his army pension. Stepping outside the railway station, he thought, 'This is probably the last train journey of my life.'

His mind went back to his last day with his unit. The Commanding Officer himself had addressed the gathering organized for his farewell on the eve of his retirement: 'Subedar Lakhan was an asset to our unit. We are proud of his bravery, his commanding capability, and the discipline and dedication with which he served the army for such a long time. We will always remember him; he will be part of this unit even after his retirement.'

Lakhan felt a terrible void inside.

He remembered how he had joined the army after passing high school. There were at least a dozen people from his village in the army, but all of them had been from land-owning families. He was the first person of his caste to join the military. His father, Shambhu Teli, who owned an oil-press, didn't want him to enlist, but he had not listened to his father and had gone for the recruitment test along with some other youths from his village. He'd always had a craze for the uniform and would admire the armymen who came back to the village on leave.

His chain of thought was broken when he noticed that the boys were finding it a struggle to carry his luggage.

'How will we go from Dumri bus-stop to the village?' he asked his nephew.

'We have come on two cycles. We will strap the luggage to the carriers,' his nephew replied.

When the three of them finally reached the bus-stop they found that the bus to Dumri had not yet arrived, so they went to a nearby teashop. As they sat there sipping their tea, a small procession of people shouting slogans walked past them on the main road. The protest was lead by women demanding: 'Down with the atrocities of landlords!' 'Tillers should be reapers!' 'Down with the police administration.' The men walked behind the women, mainly peasants and labourers, brandishing sticks and red flags. Some of them carried bows and arrows. Bringing up the rear were two men holding a banner.

Lakhan Subedar read the banner. He was surprised to see that the group was from the overground political organization of the Maoists. When he'd left his village, almost twenty years ago, there had been no such organization; whatever excesses the landlords perpetrated on them had been meekly accepted by all. He came out to watch the procession and was surprised by the numbers. 'They seem to have a huge following. Where are they going?' he asked his nephew.

'To the big field opposite the railway station. Their leaders are going to address them there,' his nephew said.

'Have they made inroads into our village too?'

'Not too much yet. But they are very active across the Kareh.'

⌘

It was a forty-five minute bus drive from Puraini to Dumri. After the three of them got to Dumri Chowk, they got their bicycles from Pratap Singh's hotel, tied the luggage to the cycle-carriers and started out for Bhagatpur. The mud road to Bhagatpur was wide enough for a jeep or even a truck, but the bridge ahead was broken and one had to cycle through it or go on foot. The bridge had been built across a tributary of the Kareh that merged with it about a mile away from the bridge. In the summer, when the river was dry, bullock-carts and jeeps drove over the riverbed.

Achal Singh Mukhia had got the bridge built many years ago, when Lakhan Subedar was still in school. Back in those days, Achal Singh used to be a young and dynamic leader. His fair skin, handsome features and immaculate white kurta-pyjamas made him look distinguished. When the bridge had been inaugurated, many big officers from the district headquarters had come to Bhagatpur in jeeps and cars flashing big red lights. Afterwards, Achal Singh Mukhia had organized a lavish feast for the visiting officials and political leaders.

Lakhan Subedar used to be an active member of Achal Singh Mukhia's team, and the mukhia had been very fond of him even though he was not from a land-owning family. After he'd joined the army, Lakhan had met Mukhia only occasionally, on his annual leave. He had always been warmly received by the mukhia.

They had reached the broken bridge. The frame was intact but the iron plates of the bridge were missing. The riverbed was dry. The tyre-marks of a bullock-cart ran clear across it. Lakhan Subedar read the inauguration plaque – still intact – that bore Achal Singh Mukhia's name. The broken bridge was now beyond repair. The villagers had tried to substitute wooden planks for the iron plates but the planks had not even been able to bear the weight of a bullock-cart, and had given way.

'How is Achal Singh Mukhia?' Lakhan Subedar asked.

'He has become very old but he is still the head of the village,' his nephew replied.

Achal Singh had been the village head when Lakhan had left his village, and now, all these years later, when he'd returned, Achal Singh was still the head. Things had not changed much, Lakhan Subedar reflected – the same old mud road, the same old village school with its thatched roof, the same old village head. The only change was the protest march near the railway station. He wondered how Mukhia and his supporters felt about the fact that the lowcastes were taking out processions to voice their demands and challenging the system openly. He thought, whatever the situation in the village, he would meet Achal Singh Mukhia and get his advice about what to do after retirement.

9.

The next morning, Lakhan Subedar went to meet Achal Singh Mukhia. He wanted to take the mukhia's blessings and seek his advice before starting a fresh venture in the village. It was a warm and sunny day. Lakhan Subedar was happy to be home. He had many plans for his life after retirement but, first, he wanted to get a better understanding of the situation in the village. And there was no one better placed than Achal Singh Mukhia to advise him.

He took the shortcut from his house to Choudhary Tola, where the landowners of the village lived. The path went through a small tract of fields, which was empty because the rabi crop had recently been harvested. A few small patches of the field were green, where the men of his caste had planted some seasonal vegetables, mostly cabbage and beans. He did not meet anyone on his way to Achal Singh Mukhia's house. He thought it strange that the village was deserted at ten in the morning.

Achal Singh's house had a large veranda, reserved only for the menfolk, which was so big that fifty people could sleep there. Most of the old men in the village practically lived here. They each had their own cot. The veranda was always packed to capacity. Achal Singh Mukhia had cordoned off a small portion of the veranda and courtyard for himself. The cordoned-off room was furnished with a reclining chair on which Achal Singh Mukhia sat facing a few plastic chairs, placed there for his important guests – mostly landlords from within the village or from neighbouring villages and sundry government officials from the area. Others, who were lucky enough to gain his audience, either sat on the floor or remained standing respectfully before him.

Lakhan Subedar entered the veranda. A few old men, all of whom he knew by name, sat or were sprawled out on the charpoys. For a fleeting moment, he felt as if they were all frozen in time.

He entered the cordoned-off area. Achal Singh Mukhia sat in his usual style on the reclining chair, clad in a spotless white pyjama and kurta. He was much older now, and the lines on his fair face had grown deeper. He was lost in thought, or probably half asleep.

Lakhan Subedar was expecting the mukhia to receive him warmly. He thought they would share memories of the days when he had assisted the mukhia in organizing the inaugural function of the bridge. After all, he had once been the mukhia's loyal follower. The mukhia would no doubt be happy that he had come back to the village after serving in the army for more than twenty years and achieving the highest rank possible for a sepoy.

He knew that most villagers dared not sit before the mukhia without his permission. But after twenty years of service in the army he was out of sync with the old ways of the village. He went straight to the mukhia and bowed his head to wish him.

The mukhia squinted at him. 'Who are you?'

'I am Subedar Lakhan, and I have come back to the village after retirement.'

Mukhia recognized him all right, but said nothing. Lakhan Subedar pulled up a chair and sat down.

'How *dare* you sit in front of me? Even if you were a colonel in the army, you are a Teli in this village. You are supposed to remain standing in front of me,' the mukhia said, his face red with rage, his body shaking in anger.

Lakhan Subedar was aghast at Mukhia's reaction. He was a subedar in the army and was practically the commander of a 1000-strong fighting force. The colonel of his unit had always shown him the utmost respect and had always offered him a seat.

He stood up, the blood pounding in his head. He wanted to hit the mukhia, but he knew what would happen if he did, and restrained himself. He didn't want unnecessary trouble on the very first day of his return. He looked around. The people in the veranda were all watching him. He turned abruptly on his heel and took the short cut back to his mohalla without once looking back.

Inside, he seethed. Time had come for a change, he felt. Now he understood the reason for the protest march that he had witnessed near Puraini Railway Station. He was lost so deep in thought that he almost stepped on a dead crow lying on the foot-track. It was not a good omen. He felt he had no future in the village. He took a deep breath. The pleasant smell of the earth and the bushes did not reassure him. He sensed that something bad was going to happen to Bhagatpur.

⌘

Lakhan Subedar reached home, burying his anger deep in his heart. He went straight to the outer veranda, where the menfolk sat, and lowered himself onto a charpoy.

A short while later he heard his wife shout, 'Something's burning!' and saw her rush towards the kitchen shed. But by that time the smell of burnt daal had already spread and hung thickly in the air.

Lakhan Subedar's thoughts were momentarily distracted from his humiliation in the mukhia's courtyard. He lay down on the charpoy to ease his legs, which ached from the tension in his mind. He began thinking of paying back Mukhia in the same coin. He was so lost in thought that he didn't notice when his father came in and quietly sat on a chair next to him.

'Did you meet Mukhia?' his father asked after a long silence.

'Yes.'

'What did he say?'

He didn't reply. He didn't want to tell his father of his humiliation, but he was sure that news of it would soon spread through the village and reach his father in the shape of juicy gossip.

He remained as he was, lying on his back, and made no attempt to sit up. His mind went back to the days when he was in the last year of high school. One evening, on his way home from school he had witnessed a fight between the two factions of the village. He had always known that there were land disputes between Achal Singh Mukhia and Pratap Singh but he had not imagined that the fight could take such an ugly turn. He had watched the mukhia marching down to the open ground on the periphery of the village with his supporters. Both sides had fought a pitched battle with sticks and swords, shouting filthy abuses at each other.

He remembered hiding himself in a nearby house, not wanting to be caught between the fighting groups. Everyone in the village had closed their doors in terror. He had run home only when Mukhia and his supporters had left, having defeated Pratap Singh and his supporters. The fight had ended in the death of one of Pratap Singh's cousins. For Lakhan Subedar, this was the other abiding memory he had of Achal Singh Mukhia.

When he had passed out of school and was planning to join the army, Lakhan had come in contact with Achal Singh during the inauguration of the bridge.

Mukhia had entrusted him with the task of inviting people from neighbouring villages to the function and for making announcements on a loudspeaker so that a large number of people would turn up for the public meeting immediately after the inauguration. In those days Lakhan had shared an excellent rapport with Achal Singh Mukhia, when many others, even young boys from the landowning families, were scared of him.

After joining the army, Lakhan had not got much chance to visit home and his interaction with Mukhia had been limited to the customary exchange of pleasantries during his annual leave. Through his army career, however, he had remained totally oblivious to the affairs of his village. Still, he had not once expected Achal Singh to behave the way he had. It pained him grievously. He would never forget the humiliation he had suffered.

The smell of burnt daal had evaporated; the commotion in the kitchen had died down and the house was quiet again. Lakhan opened his eyes and saw his father sitting silently on the chair.

Lakhan Subedar's thoughts turned to Pratap Singh, Mukhia's arch-rival, who after the bloody encounter and his defeat, had left Tesri for good and settled in Dumri, his in-laws' village, where he had opened a small roadside hotel.

'How is Pratap Singh's hotel doing?' he sat up abruptly and asked his father.

'His is the only hotel in Dumri and he is doing fine,' his father replied.

Whatever the reason for Achal Singh Mukhia's behaviour with him that day, it was difficult for Lakhan to forget the humiliation he had suffered. He was determined never to meet the mukhia again and decided that he would be quite happy to assist in his downfall.

10.

Once Ramu Hajjam resumed his work at the haat his son Pawan was asked to escort him and was instructed to stay beside him through the day because Phulmani thought that Ramu Hajjam – who still tended to lapse into bouts of silence and absentmindedness – needed to be watched. So Pawan accompanied his father to the haat, staying on with him till evening for a few days. But soon Pawan realized that his father was reluctant to have him around and that he was no longer so absent-minded even though he hardly spoke.

On the fifth day Ramu Hajjam said, 'There is really no need for you to come.'

Pawan looked at his mother. He wanted her to decide whether he should go with his father or not.

Phulmani was busy preparing breakfast but had heard what Ramu said. She didn't reply at once because she didn't want to be the one to decide. In her heart of hearts she wanted Pawan to go with his father because she was still worried about Ramu Hajjam's condition.

'Why don't you take him to the haat? He will learn the trade also,' Phulmani suggested. Her tone was gentle, more in the nature of a request than an order. This surprised Pawan because three days ago his mother had been very much in charge of the affairs of the family.

'There is no need to teach him the trade. Better he learns from Murli Compounder,' Ramu Hajjam said.

For the last four days, Pawan had just sat under the neem tree near his father's shop. Ramu Hajjam hadn't allowed him to work. He had attended to all the customers himself while his son lolled under the tree, watching his father work or looking at the squirrels playing on the trunk of the tree and recreating in his mind the sequence of events that had begun with a frisky squirrel dropping a sprig on his father's hand and had ended with his father being beaten senseless for no reason.

His father's humiliation caused Pawan indescribable pain, and the idea of avenging that humiliation took deep root in his mind. He must go to Mukhdoompur, he determined, to meet those three men.

'If you are not going to the haat with your father, you can go to Murli Compounder's place,' Phulmani said as she served Ramu Hajjam and Pawan breakfast.

Father and son ate in silence. Pawan had got dressed to accompany his father to the haat but now he decided there was no rush. After his father left, he lay down on Kalavati's bed. He wanted to go to Mukhdoompur. He decided that Murli Compounder was the best person to talk to about this because he had been to all the neighbouring villages, visiting patients. He got up and announced, 'I am going to Murli's house.' His mother was at the stove. She was happy that things were getting back to normal.

⌘

When he reached Murli Compounder's residence, Pawan saw half-a-dozen boys from the village sitting in a thatch-roofed shed, reading aloud from their books. It was a big shed, open on three sides. Murli Compounder had had it built for the school he ran. Next to the school was a veranda, open on only one side, where Murli's patients waited. Behind it was a door with a rectangular piece of wood that said, 'Dr Murli, R.M.P.'. The writing on the nameplate was crude and uneven; even the words were not in line. Murli Compounder had probably written it himself. The door led into a small room where Murli saw his patients. It contained a rickety table, a chair, and two benches opposite the table.

Like all the other parents in the village, Ramu Hajjam had sent his son to the government primary school in Bhagatpur. Pawan was a bright boy but could not study there for more than a year or two because his father could not afford to buy him the books required. When Murli Compounder started his own school in Tesri, most of the people shifted their children there because it was completely free. Pawan also joined Murli's school and, being an intelligent boy, was picked by him when he finished school to assist him at the clinic.

In Murli Compounder's absence he attended to patients and administered first-aid. He had learnt what medicines to prescribe for common ailments. Taking note of Murli Compounder's reputation and growing wealth, Ramu Hajjam had felt it was better that his son learn some medical tricks from him, rather than pursue the family profession.

After waiting for some time in the hall, Pawan walked right into the clinic. Murli Compounder sat on his chair, his stethoscope, which he liked to flaunt, prominently displayed on the table in front of him. Two villagers sat on the bench opposite him. Pawan knew them – a middle-aged woman called Shanti, and her son. The room smelt of disinfectant. Pawan sat on the other bench.

'Will this ever be cured?' Shanti had goitre.

'Not unless you stop drinking water from the Kareh,' Murli said.

'Where else can we go for water? Most times, there is no water even there. Most of the year it is dry and we have to dig the dry riverbed to get water.'

'And iodized salt is not available here; even if it were, one couldn't afford it.' Murli Compounder shook his head.

'So there is no medicine for this?'

'No. The disease will remain with you till you die.'

Shanti Devi and her son got up. Her son opened the door and the nameplate rattled against it. On cue, the children chanting their lesson in the adjacent hall increased their pitch.

'Why didn't you give her any medicine?' Pawan asked after they had left. It was the first time he had seen Murli send a patient away without medicine.

'There is no medicine for goitre. Actually, for most of our patients, diseases go away only when they die,' Murli replied, looking meaningfully at Pawan as he put away his stethoscope in his plastic bag.

Abruptly Pawan changed the subject. 'Have you ever been to Mukhdoompur?'

'No, but I have been to a village nearby called Birni.'

'How does one get there?'

Murli picked up a cloth duster and started wiping the table. 'Why do you want to go there?'

'I have some work.'

'It is three miles from here, across the Kareh. Go straight to Shyampur and then ask anyone, they will tell you the way. But, remember, these are dangerous villages, the main bastion of the Maoists. Even the police don't go there. Of course the Maoists will not harm you,' Murli said over his shoulder as he walked out of the room.

Pawan remained in the clinic, thinking about what Murli had said.

11.

Pawan didn't tell anyone that he was thinking of going to Mukhdoompur. For two days he debated the decision, but the squirrel playing on the neem tree haunted him. And then, there was his father's face, deeply drawn, as if lost in some unknown anxiety, which had made him question his very existence. There finally was a way to avenge his father's humiliation – the three men who had come to his father's shop had said as much – but that road was difficult. And it was one from which there was no turning back.

Still, something in Pawan urged him to go to Mukhdoompur, come what may. He didn't speak to his father or mother. He was inordinately quiet at home, almost as though he too had been beaten up in the haat for no fault of his and was suffering the same trauma as his father. After two days, he decided that he would go to Mukhdoompur, secretly, without telling anyone.

That day Pawan sat down to breakfast only after Ramu Hajjam had left for the haat. His grandmother sat on the veranda with him, gazing silently into the distance. When he finished his breakfast, he said to his mother, 'I am going to Birni to give a patient some medicine. If I get late, I will stay there overnight. Else, I will be back by late evening.'

Phulmani looked at him in disbelief. She knew that Murli Compounder often went to the surrounding villages but, so far, he had never deputed Pawan to go instead of him. Still, she decided to give Pawan the benefit of doubt. 'Why didn't you tell your father about this?' she asked.

'I thought he would get unnecessarily worried.' Pawan went inside the room and took out a chador, thinking it might come in handy if he had to spend the night in Mukhdoompur.

'Try to come home by evening. Otherwise your father will get very worried,' Phulmani said.

Pawan heard his mother but didn't answer her. He was already thinking about the journey ahead, and about the three men of Mukhdoompur who had not even told him their names. He was also thinking of what he would say if somebody asked him why he was going there. He wanted to avoid bumping into anyone and he was fortunate that nobody was sitting under the banyan tree that day.

Just as he thought he would get away without anyone accosting him, Chedi Paswan, the village watchman – the only government employee in the village – suddenly emerged from the opposite direction. Chedi Paswan was an elderly man. He wore the government-sanctioned uniform – blue shirt, red turban and white dhoti – and always carried a stick with which he used to hit the ground or walls as he patrolled, creating enough clatter to wake the dead. Once a week, he visited the police station to brief the officer about the happenings in his area. Both Bhagatpur and Tesri fell under his jurisdiction but he spent more time in Bhagatpur where the rich and influential resided. He came to Tesri, where he was from, only to sleep during the day.

Having spotted Pawan, Chedi Paswan stopped for a moment, took his turban in his hand and hit his stick on the ground. Then he stood there with his head tilted to one side, looking completely exhausted.

'Where are you going?' he asked.

'Towards the river,' Pawan replied.

'Don't go across the river. The area is unsafe.'

'For the police maybe – not for people like us.'

Pawan's reply surprised the watchman. He looked at him intently as he took a deep breath and put his turban back on his head. 'If they are your friends, then the police is your enemy,' he said before setting off again, hitting his stick hard on the ground with each step, in the way he did at night to warn off thieves.

⌘

Crossing the Kareh did not prove too difficult since it was a vast riverbed without heavy water flow. At some places there was ankle- to knee-deep water, and

Pawan waded through easily. Once he crossed the river he was relieved that he would now not meet any one he knew. After walking a while he saw a village just ahead. From what Murli Compounder had told him, he knew it to be Shyampur. He saw a couple of boys playing under a sprawling banyan tree similar to the one in Tesri. The boys were not much younger than him. For a moment he felt as if he were back home. He realized that the colour of want is the same everywhere.

'Which way to Mukhdoompur?' he asked one of the boys, all of whom had stopped playing and were staring at him.

'Go to the end of this village and keep on walking for an hour. You will reach a bigger village. That is Mukhdoompur,' the boy said.

An hour later Pawan could see the village in the distance. The sun was shining overhead and it was very hot. To enter Mukhdoompur, one had to climb a narrow dirt track between two hillocks. Walking up he wiped his brow and stared down at the village, spread out as if on a saucer. House after house of thatched roof and mud walls. There was no orderliness to them. Beyond the village he saw a long stretch of elephant grass. He stood there on the narrow pass and considered what to do. How would he ever find the three men who had come to his father's shop? He knew that he could not go around openly asking for them.

Suddenly, two young men who seemed to materialize out of nowhere, stopped him in his tracks. He realized with a start that they must have been keeping watch on the village. Both of them looked quite young, maybe a couple of years older than him. One sported a beard and had a scar above his left eyebrow.

'Where do you want to go?' the bearded one asked.

'Mukhdoompur,' Pawan mumbled.

'This is Mukhdoompur. Why are you here?'

Pawan thought for a moment. 'I am Pawan from Tesri,' he said. 'My father is a barber and works in the Bhagatpur haat. He was beaten up for no reason by the landlords of Bhagatpur. A few days later three men came to my father's shop. They said they could help us get justice. They said we should come here. I want to meet them.' Pawan spoke with a confidence he did not feel.

One of them took Pawan aside, frisked him and then asked him to follow them. The one with the beard walked ahead, and the other right behind Pawan. The village was not very far from the hillock. When they reached the first house in the settlement, the bearded man asked Pawan to wait outside it. After a few minutes he came out from the house accompanied by a tall man in a kurta-pyjama with a cotton towel on his shoulder. The man introduced himself as Murti and asked the same questions that the two young boys had asked him. He wanted to be sure that Pawan was really who he said he was.

'Do you know anyone from Tesri?' Murti asked.

'Jamuna Das. He is our village head,' Pawan promptly replied.

Murti was satisfied with this response and asked

Pawan to wait on a wooden bench under a guava tree. Pawan did as he was instructed. There were ripe guavas hanging on the branches. Pawan was hungry and wanted to pick one, but then he thought it wouldn't be proper. He had a feeling Murti was still keeping an eye on him.

Pawan began to feel very apprehensive. The silence there was unnatural. Only a small blackbird shrilled intermittently from the branches of the tree. He wondered why the village looked so deserted. So far, he had seen only three people – two near the hillock and one after entering the village. He felt increasingly uneasy. But then he saw a group of women winding their way down the hillock to the village, carrying bundles of grass on their heads, and he relaxed. He waited, suppressing his urge to eat the fleshy, yellow guava. Other birds joined the lone blackbird and started making trilling noises.

An hour went by. A cyclist passed by on the main road, reminding him of Murli Compounder. Another group of women went towards the field. Sitting there, Pawan suddenly realized that life here was no different from that in his own village.

Finally, Murti emerged from the room and Pawan took the opportunity to ask for some water to drink because his throat felt parched. Murti led him to the rear of the house, where there was a hand-pump. He worked the pump while Pawan drank water directly from the pipe. Then Pawan came back to the bench and continued watching the birds pecking at the ripe guavas. After another hour, Murti came out with a plate of rice and vegetables and set it on the bench beside Pawan.

'Have something to eat. You can get water from the hand pump. After you finish we will go to meet the people you have come to see,' he said and went away.

Pawan enjoyed every morsel of the food as he was ravenous after his three-mile-long walk.

After a while, Murti returned, 'Let us go. They are waiting for you,' he said.

The two of them walked a short distance and reached a house in the middle of the village. It was also a mud house, but it was bigger than the first one. It had a small veranda, covered with a palm-thatched roof on bamboo poles. Two wooden benches stood in the veranda. Again Pawan was instructed to wait. After some time, a young man came out of the room. He was bare-chested, his torso loosely draped in a grey shawl. Pawan recognized him immediately. He was one of the three men who had visited his father's shop. He got up, but the man indicated to him to remain seated and sat down on the bench facing him.

'How is your father?' he asked.

'He is better now.'

'I am glad you have come. We should not accept injustice without challenging it. All through the ages, we have suffered so much. We have to take up arms against the oppressors, the exploiters who have taken over our fields, our rights.'

Pawan listened intently. He was confused for a moment, but he wanted to know more about the organization. 'What can your organization do to ensure justice for poor people like us?' Pawan asked.

'We fight against injustice. We want to ensure equal rights for every person of this country. We believe in using the barrel of the gun to bring an end to the exploitation of the poor by the rich and influential. We wish to spread our area of influence by involving the poor and downtrodden people throughout the country in our struggle. Soon, in the course of time, we will have the Maoist flag flying in Delhi. We have already liberated a large part of the country from the exploitative machinery of the government which runs by means of the nexus between the landlords and the capitalists of our society.'

Pawan did not understand half of what the man was saying but he was impressed with the sentiment. 'What will I have to do if I join your organization?' he asked.

'You will be sent to a training camp. After that, we will see what responsibility should be assigned to you, depending on your capability. Of course you will have to leave your village and family since the police will be after you. They are with the landlords. We have to fight against them as well. And it is a big mission because we fight for the cause of all the poor, oppressed people of the world. One day we hope to create a society free from exploitation, where there will be equal distribution of property and nobody will dare to do what they did to your father.'

Murti stood with him, listening carefully as if he had never heard this speech before. 'Where are the other two men who had come with you to the haat?' Pawan asked innocently.

'They have gone somewhere, for other missions. We are not supposed to know about each others' programme.'

Pawan was overwhelmed by the gravity of the situation. He was very impressed by the Maoists' discipline and their commitment to the cause. From the looks of them they seemed like simple, regular folk.

In the distance, children played. Pawan watched them. They had fashioned a football out of old rags and were kicking it with their bare feet, the way the children in his village played.

'There is no hurry. You can think over it and come back to us. We don't force anybody. You may go back to your village. But don't tell anybody about us. We are not kind to informants,' the man said.

This made it easy for Pawan, because he was going to ask for permission to go back to his village. He looked at the sky. If he started now, he would be able to cross the Kareh before sunset. As he got up to leave, the man said, 'If you come back, go to the same house where you had been taken earlier today.'

Pawan started on the long trek home to his village. Murti escorted him up to the narrow road between the hillocks. After that he was alone. He looked back at Mukhdoompur. The village was hidden from view behind a thicket. He looked at the bushes and suddenly felt as if the bushes were alive with people; as though he was being closely watched. He walked briskly down the narrow dirt road, flanked on both sides by recently reaped fields. He continued on against the slanting sun rays and amidst the continuous chirping of the birds. When he crossed the riverbed the sun had become an orange ball hanging on the horizon. His feet sank inside the stream where there was knee-deep water. He let his feet sink further, bowed down, filled water in his hollowed palm and drank till his thirst was quenched. In front of him, his village was visible. He wondered how often he would be able to come home once he joined the organization.

12.

Summer arrived, giving the fields around Lakhan Subedar's house a dry and wasted look. Dust-laden winds fanned the heat everywhere. Lying in his charpoy, Lakhan Subedar could not expel the memory of his humiliating encounter with Achal Singh Mukhia from his mind. Nothing had prepared him for the crushing put-down. Twenty years in the army had only inflated his ego. There, he had commanded respect because of his position and hard work. Mukhia had damaged his self-esteem beyond repair. He had been made painfully aware of his lowly status. Lakhan Subedar could think of nothing but revenge.

For two days, he was so disturbed he didn't know what to do with himself; he could not decide what to do and where to go. He couldn't bring himself to step out of his house and, remained prone, glued to the charpoy in his veranda. He remembered his days in the army. Living in the village after retirement was not the idyllic life he had imagined.

The village had changed, and the change was for the worse.

Everywhere, there were factions. People were against each other, conspiring in smaller and smaller groups. He had come home to his village thinking he would live with his parents and do something for the betterment of his people. But now he was regretting not settling down in the city like some of his other colleagues had.

His thoughts were interrupted when he saw his wife coming to the veranda, her head covered with the edge of her sari.

'It has been more than three days since you went to meet the Mukhia, and you have barely stirred from your charpoy since,' she said.

He didn't reply and fixed his gaze on the semal tree across his house that had turned green after shedding all its flowers. The semal was his favourite tree, and he would often think of it during his long absences from the village. He knew its routine well: flowering in the month of March, blossoming with big, red flowers that fell one by one by the end of April, to be eaten by the village cattle. After that the tree would turn green with fruit, which would mature and burst open in May, releasing wisps of feathery cotton that floated in the air and travelled quite far, even crossing into neighbouring villages.

'You haven't left this cot for the last two days. Are you worried about the future because we have no children?' she asked again.

He looked intently at his wife. She had raised this issue so many times that by now he had become used to her guilt-ridden reproaches. He had tried his best – taken her to the most reputed doctors and had himself thoroughly checked – but despite it all they had remained childless. His wife was ravaged by her own sense of inadequacy and battled occasional bouts of depression.

'My troops were my children. But here I have to do something to kill time.' He didn't tell her the real reason for his distress.

'So what will you do now?' she asked.

But before Lakhan Subedar could reply, his father came into the veranda. Immediately, his wife pulled her pallu over her head and scurried back inside. Lakhan Subedar got off the cot and went and sat on the chair lying next to it. A gust of the dust-laden wind had left a layer of grime everywhere on the veranda. Neither father nor son spoke for a long time.

'I will go to Dumri to see Pratap Singh,' Lakhan Subedar finally said.

'Are you planning some venture with him?' his father asked.

'Yes. I am planning to buy a mini bus to ply on the Dumri–Puraini road. He will be helpful because he owns a hotel at Dumri Chowk.'

'You should be careful. Pratap Singh is Mukhia's arch-enemy,' his father said.

Lakhan Subedar did not say that this was precisely why he wished to get closer to Pratap Singh. Only Pratap Singh could challenge the supremacy of

Achal Singh Mukhia. Lakhan knew about the long-standing dispute between the two families and had a vivid memory of the fight he had witnessed. He knew that Pratap had lost out to the growing clout and power of Achal Singh Mukhia, when the latter became politically important in the area. Realizing that support for him was waning, Pratap Singh had left the village and settled down in Dumri. People from his community declared him an out-caste, but they knew that Pratap Singh was still strong in some ways.

Before he set out to meet Pratap Singh, Lakhan informed his wife that he might stay overnight at Dumri. He wanted to have a long talk with Pratap Singh in private.

At three-thirty that afternoon, Lakhan left for Pratap Singh's teashop. It was a windy afternoon. It would take him around two hours to reach there, which meant he could technically get there before the sun set.

When he reached Dumri Chowk, a bus had just pulled into the station. The paint on its body was so faded that it was difficult to say what its original colour had been. The bus conductor was calling passengers in a high-pitched voice – '*Puraini. Puraini.* Last bus for *Puraini.*' A few passengers continued to stand where they were, oblivious to his calls. Only when the driver went into the bus and started revving the engine did they scramble to clamber aboard. Some, who didn't fit inside, hung on to the ladder at the back of the bus.

After the bus left, an uneasy quiet descended on the bus-stop. A lone man sat at the paan shop. The cycle-repair man was packing his tools and closing shop for the day. Two stray dogs goofed around with each other.

Lakhan Subedar went straight to Pratap Singh's teashop. Pratap Singh sat on a cot, with a small wooden box in which he kept his bills, lying next to him. Seeing Lakhan Subedar, he got up and offered him a seat.

Lakhan noticed that Pratap Singh had aged, but in spite of the wrinkles on his face and the sparse white hair on his head, his face glowed. Lakhan estimated that Pratap Singh would be about fifteen years older than him.

'Namaskar, Subedar. Have you come back to the village to live here?' Pratap Singh enquired.

'Yes, but the village has become so different. It has changed for the worse,' Lakhan Subedar said.

'It is worsening day by day. It is no longer the village you had left twenty years ago.'

'How do you live here, in the middle of nowhere?' Lakhan Subedar changed the topic.

Pratap Singh looked around thoughtfully. Three customers in the shop were having tea and samosas. Their bicycles were parked outside. They had arrived on the last bus and were having something to eat before they rode back to their village. Lakhan Subedar didn't know who they were. He had been cut off from the village for so long that he barely recognized anyone from the younger lot.

Pratap Singh went to a room behind the teashop. The three customers paid their bill and went on their way. When Pratap Singh returned from the room, the sun had set, and the darkness and silence around had grown thicker.

'There will be no more customers now. Prepare some tea and dinner for us. Subedar will be staying overnight,' Pratap Singh instructed the small boy who did odd jobs around the place.

Then the two men sat outside sipping their tea till the moon rose in the sky. It was not so dark outside because of the bright moonlight.

'There is one last bus coming from Puraini, at around seven-thirty. Only a few passengers from Dumri village come by that bus since their village is not far,' Pratap Singh said.

'Don't you go back to Dumri for the night?' Lakhan Subedar asked.

'No, sometimes I spend the night here.'

'Is it safe?'

'I have no fear. The people are with me,' Pratap Singh said.

The last bus from Puraini arrived on schedule. There was a sudden burst of activity at the bus-stop. Three people got off the bus, but they didn't stop at the teashop and went straight on to Dumri. Then the whole place became quiet again. Not even a dog barked. The metalled road shone in the moonlight. The errand-boy was putting the finishing touches to their meal and, after a while, set out the plates on the charpoy. When they finished their dinner, the boy unrolled two sets of bedding on the charpoys for Pratap Singh and Lakhan Subedar and then went to sleep. Pratap Singh and Lakhan Subedar sat and chatted for a long time about Bhagatpur, about the growing strength of the Maoists in the area and about Lakhan Subedar's army days.

Late in the night, three men came to the hotel from across the road. Seeing them there, at that hour, Lakhan Subedar was alarmed for a moment but he soon realized that Pratap Singh knew them. They sat on an empty charpoy opposite Pratap Singh's bed and viewed Lakhan Subedar suspiciously. Pratap Singh shouted for the small errand-boy to wake up and make tea for everybody.

'Who is your guest today?' one of the men asked, indicating Lakhan.

'Lakhan Subedar – a retired army subedar. He is from my village. He has recently retired from the army and wants to start some work. He is our sympathizer. You don't have to worry about him,' Pratap Singh replied.

'What work do you want to start?' the man asked Lakhan Subedar.

'I want to buy a minibus to ply on the Dumri–Puraini route,' Lakhan Subedar replied.

'No bus runs on this road without our permission. But we will help you because you are a friend of Pratap Singh.'

Lakhan Subedar looked at the man closely. He had a chubby face, a thick black moustache and wore a cotton gamcha around his neck. His looks and demeanour were that of an upper-caste landowner. This surprised Lakhan Subedar. Were these people Maoists or were they supporters of people like Achal Singh Mukhia? He thought it prudent not to ask.

'Do the policemen still come to your shop?' one of the other men asked Pratap Singh.

'Yes, but only during the day,' Pratap Singh replied.

'Good. That means the police is scared of us. We have forced them to remain indoors during the night. We are going to start a fresh offensive against the landlords of this area. They will be forced to flee their lands and we will distribute their land among the poor,' the third man said.

After finishing their tea the three strangers followed Pratap Singh into the room behind the teashop. Lakhan Subedar remained where he was. He saw two of the men standing at the entrance of the teashop, keeping a watch on the road. He realized that people's motives for joining the Maoists were different. Pratap Singh was supporting them because he had been bested by Achal Singh Mukhia. Since the Maoists had become the arch rivals of Achal Singh, Pratap Singh had started conspiring with them.

Of the three men, two had looked distinctly upper-caste. He knew then that though his reasons for coming to meet Pratap Singh were very personal, eventually he would also be supporting the Maoists.

Pratap Singh and his mysterious visitors remained closeted in the room for a long time. They left the teashop in the early hours of the morning, as the owls hooted in the trees. Watching them leave, Lakhan Subedar decided that he would, after all, not run a mini bus service on the Dumri–Puraini stretch. That would put him at the mercy of both the Maoists and the police.

13.

When he first ran away to join the Maoists, nobody in the village commented on Pawan's absence. They thought he was just one of the many 'runaway boys' of the village who had fled to the city to earn a better living. Then, by and by, rumours that he had joined hands with the Maoists, gained strength. The villagers were shocked. Soon everyone was talking about it.

Ramu Hajjam realized the significance of his son joining the Maoists only when Chedi Paswan, the village chowkidar, knocked on his door one evening. The sight of Chedi Paswan alarmed him. In the dim yellow light of the lantern hanging on the doorway, Chedi Paswan's face looked grimmer than ever.

Ramu Hajjam was sitting on his charpoy in the courtyard, having just returned from the haat. All that he knew was that around a week ago his son had left home without informing his mother of his plans and that there had been no news of him since. Like everyone else, he'd assumed that Pawan had left the village to earn his livelihood and, sooner or later, would send information of his whereabouts.

'Do you know your son has gone underground with the Maoists?' Chedi asked.

Ramu Hajjam was dumbfounded. He had not heard the talk doing the rounds in the village.

'I have no clue. He did not tell us when he was going. We assumed he had gone to Kolkata to find work. What can we do if he has gone underground?' he said.

Chedi Paswan sank down on the cot with his shoulders drooping and his head lowered and wheezed loudly. Ramu Hajjam could not understand why Chedi Paswan looked so pained. The lantern flickered for a moment. The agony on the chowkidar's face was evident even in the dim light of the lantern.

'He is the first person to join the Maoists from this side of the Kareh,' the chowkidar said morosely.

For Ramu Hajjam, till that time, his son's running away had been important; his joining the Maoists, not so much. Now he began to worry about the impact his son's joining the Maoists would have. 'This is going to start an exodus. If one joins them, others will follow and that will bring misfortune all around. You must go and call him back. It will be best for everybody.'

'If you want me to I will try,' Ramu Hajjam assured him.

⌘

That night, after Chedi Paswan left, the full import of Pawan's going underground dawned on Ramu Hajjam and his wife. Only then, did they understand why Pawan had been so silent that past week, why he had looked so lost in thought. Both of them were anxious. Their only son had disappeared, and now the police and the landlords of Bhagatpur were after him. They sat there with heavy hearts and feared sharing the information with Kalavati. They didn't move even when Kalavati called. Finally, when the flickering lantern breathed its last, they went to bed without eating.

Ramu Hajjam decided to go to Mukhdoompur and bring Pawan home. He was sure his son would not refuse him.

Lying in bed Ramu Hajjam whispered to his wife, 'I will go tomorrow to find him and try to get him back.'

Phulmani said nothing.

She knew she had already lost her son.

⌘

Early the next morning, Ramu Hajjam went to see Murli Compounder. 'Where can I find Pawan? He has been gone for a week.'

'It won't be difficult to find him but it will be difficult to bring him home because as far as I know he has gone forever.' There was an air of certainty in Murli Compounder's voice. Then he told Ramu that Pawan had been asking him for directions to Mukhdoompur.

Ramu Hajjam set off for Mukhdoompur immediately, directly from Murli Compounder's house – past the Kareh, past the nondescript village on the way where the boys played and buffaloes wallowed in the mud. He continued to walk till he reached the hillocks. He didn't need to ask anyone for directions as he had travelled to all the villages around Tesri with his father. As he crossed the hillock, just before entering the village precinct of Mukhdoompur, he was waylaid by two men, in much the same manner his son had been stopped a few days ago.

'Where do you want to go?' they asked.

'To the village, to see my son.'

They asked him to unwrap his chador and raise his arms over his head and then they searched him.

Ramu Hajjam's mind raced impatiently as he was being frisked. He was desperate to see his son. 'Take me to my son. I want to talk to him alone. Can I talk to him privately?' he wanted to know though he didn't know whether these were the right people to talk to.

He was taken to the same house to which his son had first been taken. The guava tree was laden with ripe fruit. One of the men stayed back to keep watch on him while the other went aside. Fortunately he was not made to wait long.

The man standing outside beckoned him. 'Follow me. I will take you to your son.'

Ramu Hajjam followed him without any urgency as if, now, he was sure that his son would come back to Tesri with him. He passed through the narrow streets of the village, amidst mud houses with thatched roofs and found himself in a small courtyard. Ahead of him was a room that opened on to a veranda. Inside, three middle-aged men were seated on a rug. The house smelled of cut grass.

Ramu Hajjam did not see his son among them and felt frustrated. 'Why don't you let me see my son?' he asked the man who had led him in. One of the men sitting inside the room answered, 'Your son is with us but he has come here of his own volition. We did not force him to stay.'

'I want to meet him. He is my son.'

'He is your son but he has decided to fight with us against the atrocities of people like Subedar Singh. You can take him back if he decides to go. We do not force anybody to stay with us.'

Ramu Hajjam didn't reply. He had no answer. The unbearable anxiety of waiting was getting to him.

They asked him to sit down. He was tired and thirsty as he had been walking since morning. A glass of water was brought for him.

'How long will you people grovel? We could have easily avenged your humiliation by killing Subedar Singh, but we want you people to fight for yourself. Your son has come here to fight for bringing about a change in society. But if he wants to return with you, we have no problem.'

The man asked loudly for Pawan to be sent in. Ramu Hajjam fixed his gaze on the door on the other side of the room, desperate to see his son who had left home a week ago. The next moment Pawan appeared at the door. Ramu Hajjam got up and moved towards

Pawan, held his hand and looked into his eyes. There was a new assurance and maturity in his son's face – as if he had grown seven years in the last seven days.

Ramu Hajjam's hands were trembling, his eyes were full of tears. He legs gave way under him and he sank down on his haunches. Pawan sat down with him, facing his father. Everybody present in the room looked at them. A heavy silence hung inside the room.

After a long silence, Ramu Hajjam said, 'Your mother is waiting for you, son. Come back home.'

'I have not run away from the village. I have come here for a purpose and I will go back to the village only when I avenge your humiliation and all the other atrocities we have been suffering for ages at the hands of the landlords of Bhagatpur. I cannot go back without finishing my work, Baba,' Pawan replied.

Ramu Hajjam knew suddenly that the equation between them had changed; he could no longer order his son about. He felt like shouting: 'You *have* to come with me. You *have* to come with me,' but he could not. His voice caught in his throat. Somehow he controlled himself and said, 'You are our only reason for living. Your mother will die without you.'

'I will come to see her whenever I can, but I cannot leave this work,' Pawan looked away from his father's eyes.

Ramu Hajjam was speechless. He felt an inexplicable pain in his stomach. He looked at his son intently. As he stood up he said: 'As long as we are alive, we are there for you. But don't let us get humiliated either by the police or by the landlords of Bhagatpur.'

He left Mukhdoompur amidst the maze of houses, walking disconsolately through the narrow alleys, past the hillocks and past the nondescript villages on the way. All the while he felt as if someone was following him. When he reached the vast riverbed of Kareh, he could not stop himself from looking back, in the improbable hope that his son had followed him. But only the long and wide riverbed of Kareh stared back at him. He felt the soft golden sand of the river sift under his bare feet.

Ramu Hajjam sank down into the sand. He wanted to wail, 'Pawan! Come back! Come back, son! We are bereft without you!' But his voice failed him and he lay back in the soft sand and wished that a strong current of water would wash over him and carry him away to a far-away place, so distant that nobody would even be able to identify his dead body.

He lay there, his throat dry and parched, and started to dream.

⌘

In his dream, Ramu saw a great saint with a halo around his head and a shining face that reflected absolute peace. The saint sat on a high pedestal adorned with beautiful carvings and a king stood before him with his head bent.

The saint asked the king, 'Why have you come here, Your Majesty?'

And the king said, 'I saw a dream early in the morning. And when I told my state purohit and some other brahmins about it, they said that the dream foretold evil. That sacrifices were required to avert calamity. I want to know the meaning of my dream.'

And the saint said, 'Tell me about your dream, Your Majesty.'

And the king said: 'I saw in my dream a very handsome warrior wearing all kinds of weapons on his body leading a hundred horsemen but the warrior refused to fight in the war, instead he ran inside a jungle and did not come outside even after hearing the powerful beat of the war drum. But, on the other hand, I saw an ordinary man having no weapon on his body except a club, declaring war against the king and his unrighteous men. The dream terrified me. Tell me, what does it mean?'

And the saint replied that in the days to come, the kings will be unrighteous and unjust. Nobody will listen to the grievances of poor people. The king's men and loyalists will unleash a reign of injustice. Then, the ordinary people will start fighting for their own cause as, in the dream, the ordinary person took the leadership, declaring war against the unrighteous king whereas the warrior of high kshatriya caste refused to move.

And the king asked, 'When will this happen?'

And the saint said, 'Not in your reign, your majesty. You rule with righteousness. This will come to pass in the distant future.'

And Ramu Hajjam heard himself almost shouting, 'The time has come! Look at my son, the son of an ordinary barber. He has run away, all alone, to fight his own battle, to fight against the humiliation his father has suffered. Look at him! And he refuses to come back!'

And Ramu Hajjam wanted to ask the saint when his son would come back but then he saw in his dream that the king and the saint were no longer there. He started running to find them, but total darkness engulfed him and he woke up and felt the soft sand of the riverbed on which he lay. He heard the chirping of birds and the sound of the shallow stream of water flowing not far from him. He felt thirsty and went towards the stream. After drinking a few handfuls of water, he started for Tesri.

He knew that Pawan would never come back.

Never.

14.

Lakhan Subedar had never expected life after retirement to be so difficult. After his run-in with the mukhia, he had stopped going to Choudhary Tola altogether. There was no one to talk to in his neighbourhood except the people from his own community and a few families from the lowcastes. He had little to say to them and their stupid questions about his life in the army only irritated him further. He felt lonely in the village, and sat on his veranda all day. After meeting Pratap Singh, and having met the Maoists at the teashop, he had all but dropped the idea of buying a minibus.

A few weeks later, on a hot afternoon when the sun seemed to hang endlessly on the horizon, he walked through the bamboo grove by the old canal road that passed along the Kareh, and crossed over, into Tesri. He went straight to the platform under the banyan tree in the centre of the village where the men sat. A couple of boys were trying to settle the dust and cool the hot earth by sprinkling water on the ground around the platform. Jamuna Das was there too, standing beside his famous radio. The village cattle was returning home, kicking up more dust along the way.

'Namaskar!' Jamuna Das, stood up on seeing Lakhan and folded his hands. As he got up his dhoti, which was caught under the radio, brought the radio crashing down to the ground. The shell of the radio cracked open revealing its innards and scattering the batteries about.

'Namaskar,' Lakhan Subedar replied, as a young boy got down on his haunches and started retrieving the batteries.

'It is a very old radio and stops working quite often. So it speaks as infrequently as I do,' Jamuna Das laughed, trying to cover his embarrassment.

'It must be the only source of information for you people. I remember when I was deployed in difficult locations in high-altitude areas during my army days, the radio was our only means of entertainment. It kept our sanity intact,' Lakhan said and sat down on the mud platform next to Jamuna Das.

'We get to know what's happening in our area through this radio,' one of the men in the gathering offered.

'What do you mean? Does the radio give news about our region too?' Lakhan Subedar asked.

'Yes – about the Maoists who have complete control over the area across the Kareh. Particularly when major incidents occur, like any police action or killings by the Maoists,' the man replied.

'Do they have a support base this side of the river as well?' Lakhan Subedar enquired.

'A boy from our village has recently gone underground with them. God knows how many will follow suit.'

Everyone grew quiet on hearing this, as if they did not want to accept the fact. They watched the young man who had picked up the batteries, trying to re-assemble the radio, but it refused to show any signs of life. The birds on the banyan tree started chirping loudly, as if to fill the silence. The boy hit the radio a few times hoping that it would start functioning but nothing happened. He got up and laughed. 'Sometimes merely whacking it makes it work, but today it is quite dead,' he declared.

'Without the radio we will start relying on gossip and get to hear half-baked stories about the Maoists from across the river,' a middle-aged man said.

Lakhan Subedar decided then and there to give his radio to them and buy himself a new one from the army canteen.

Jamuna Das had remained quiet all this while, listening to the others speak and gauging Lakhan Subedar's reactions to what they said. He wanted to understand why Lakhan Subedar had come to his village. 'Leave the subject of the Maoists aside. Has anyone even asked Lakhan Subedar whether he wants a glass of water?' Jamuna Das intervened.

The young man who was handling the radio got up to get a glass of water but Lakhan Subedar interrupted, 'Thanks. I don't want any water right now.'

'You have returned to your village after retirement. How do you feel about coming home, Subedar?' Jamuna Das asked.

Lakhan Subedar was surprised Jamuna Das knew of his retirement. 'I feel a little unsettled because the village is not the way it was when I left it more than twenty years ago.'

'Yes, it has changed a lot from those old days,' Jamuna Das agreed. 'But I do not know whether it is for better or worse. I am an old man and have seen the old days when none of us from this village dared even stand before the landowners of Bhagatpur. Now the people of Bhagatpur are scared to even cross the Kareh. Some big landlords have even abandoned their lands across the river.'

Lakhan Subedar thought of Achal Singh Mukhia. These new developments did not augur well for Achal Singh. He felt happy. He reflected on the status of his own caste in the village order. He realized that being from the business caste it had never been so bad for him. Some members of his caste were economically better off than the smaller landholders of Bhagatpur. But there was no question of them being accorded an equal social status.

'Yes, nobody can stop change,' he said, also thinking of the long protest march he had seen on his arrival at the Puraini Railway Station. 'Now the poor people have taken up arms against the landowners.'

'But nobody knows to what all this will lead. And I don't know whether spilling blood is worth the price of anything,' Jamuna Das said.

Lakhan Subedar sat and chatted for a long time. Only when the muezzin from the thatched-roof mosque of Kunjra Toli called out did Lakhan Subedar get up and take their permission to leave.

That was not the last time Lakhan Subedar came there to chat with the villagers of Tesri to find out exactly what was happening in the village. He gifted his radio to them and sat with them regularly. And he paid no attention when Chedi Paswan whispered: 'Why do you sit with them? The landlords of Bhagatpur do not like it.'

15.

Almost everyone in Tesri initially thought that Pawan would not be able to survive the Maoists and would return to the village in a week or two. But when he did not come back after a month, the villagers realized he was serious about his plans; that he had, in fact, actually gone underground with the Maoists.

One evening, not long after Pawan's departure, the villagers were sitting under the banyan tree as usual. It was hot and windy outside, but the villagers had gathered under the tree because it was even more unbearable indoors.

As they sat there Chedi Paswan shuffled up to the gathering. Normally he never sat and chatted with the villagers and avoided discussing village issues with them. As the only representative of the government in the village, he felt it necessary to impress his importance upon them. He preferred to spend his time in Bhagatpur where the influential people resided – people who had direct access to the officers of the police station and whose adverse feedback could land him in serious trouble.

But that day, to everybody's surprise, he walked straight to the platform under the banyan tree limping in that peculiar way of his; his body-weight listing to the left, walking with the aid of the staff he always carried. He reached the platform and sat down with such dejection that Jamuna Das asked, 'Is everything okay with you?'

The chowkidar removed his red turban and placed it on the platform. 'I wish it was,' he wheezed.

Nobody spoke for a while. Jamuna Das was always careful when talking to Chedi Paswan because he knew that Chedi would pass on anything he said to the landlords of Bhagatpur, particularly to Achal Singh Mukhia.

'I visited the police station last week and the officer in charge yelled at me. "How could somebody from your village join the Maoists?" he said. My job is gone now. Achal Singh Mukhia doesn't trust me. He thinks that I will help the Maoists because I am from this village. I don't know what to do,' Chedi Paswan said, coughing as he spoke.

For the first time in his life, Jamuna Das believed him. And for the first time, the villagers realized how serious the matter was and how grave its consequences could be.

'We are not responsible for Pawan's actions nor can we compel him to come back,' Jamuna Das said.

'I know nobody can bring him back. I have already told Ramu Hajjam to try and bring his son home. But even though he went there to get him, Pawan refused to return to Tesri,' the chowkidar said.

Everyone looked concerned.

'So what happens now?' Jamuna Das asked.

'The police will come to this village in search of Pawan, knowing fully well that he isn't here. They will come in the dead of night, they will wake us up and harass and humiliate each one of us, as though we are all personally responsible,' the chowkidar said.

Jamuna Das was distraught. He had always strived to maintain a balance between the willful youth of his village – who wanted equality for all – and the landowners of Bhagatpur who wanted to retain their dominance in the area. His efforts at keeping the conflict to a minimum had been more or less successful. But, of late, he had been finding it increasingly difficult to contain the rising ambition of the younger lot – particularly those who had come back to the village after working for a while in the big cities.

On a personal level, he had always maintained good relations with the people of Bhagatpur; had paid his respects on all appropriate occasions, and had visited Achal Singh Mukhia every now and then to pay obeisance to him. Jamuna Das was quite aghast at the disrespectful attitude of the younger generation of his village who questioned the authority of Achal Singh Mukhia and wanted equal rights with the upper-caste gentry of Bhagatpur. Jamuna Das could never have imagined things could come to this pass. Now Jamuna Das was worried that relations between the two villages would grow very tense.

'What are the people of Bhagatpur saying? What does Achal Singh Mukhia have to say?' he wanted to know.

'They are saying they will fight back if the Maoists threaten them and they will get a police camp in their village for security,' the chowkidar said.

'That means we will also have to fight back because then there is no way out,' a young man spoke up.

Jamuna Das looked at him closely. He realized that the situation would not take long to turn violent. He felt an uneasiness in the pit of his stomach.

Chedi Paswan picked up his turban – a sign of his authority as chowkidar of the village – 'Nobody is going to get anything out of this,' he rasped asthmatically.

Just then the people under the banyan tree saw Ramu Hajjam dragging his way down the main alley on his way home. His bent head, his unkempt hair and wild beard gave him a sad, dejected air.

He did not even look at the gathering.

'Has anybody thought about him and the pain he is going through? His only son has joined the Maoists. His wife is yet to recover from the shock,' Jamuna Das said.

For some time they were all silent.

Then a youth sitting next to Jamuna Das said, 'They say he has gone mad after his son left. Now he hangs a plastic sheet over his shop all the time – even during the night – and he has had a small idol of Hanumanji enshrined next to his shop; he sits in front of it when he does not have customers. God knows what kind of mantras he utters. He has delusions and talks to himself. See his dishevelled hair and wild beard? Just imagine, a barber not shaving himself!'

A bunch of birds fluttered out of the tree into the darkness. Their wild squawks brought the radio to mind. 'Let us at least listen to the radio,' someone suggested and Jamuna Das switched it on immediately, happy for the diversion.

But not before Chowkidar Chedi Paswan said, 'What I am worried about is that most of us may go through the same kind of grief that has struck Ramu Hajjam.' He put his turban on his head, picked up his stick and slowly, unsteadily, wobbled homeward.

He could sleep at night now because the fear of the Maoists had put petty crime at bay.

16.

It was the month of June. The sun beat down on the village mercilessly, forcing the people to remain indoors. The village had a deserted, desolate look.

But then the elections to the State Assembly were announced. With the announcement, the sleepy villages suddenly came alive. The peace of Bhagatpur village was shattered by the sound of a loudspeaker, fitted onto a cycle rickshaw blaring its monotonous message: 'Brothers and sisters, please give your valuable vote to the Horse symbol and help your favourite candidate win from your constituency.' And then the announcer, with a wet towel on his head to protect him from the heat, droned out high praise for the candidate, lauding the noble work he had done for the cause. Finally, when his throat dried out completely and he tired of shouting, he parked his cycle rickshaw under a tree in the middle of the village and blasted old romantic film songs – *'Kya karoon sajani, Aaye na baalam'* – from the loudspeaker, attracting a crowd of restless children hoping to kill the boredom of another hot afternoon.

The announcer was campaigning for a candidate whom no one had ever heard of. He was a young man in a lungi and shirt, his face concealed in a wet towel. The boy pulling the rickshaw was barely sixteen with sunken cheeks and an emaciated body. He was shirtless in that unbearable afternoon heat, protected only by a thin dirty cotton cloth wrapped around his neck. He braked the rickshaw under the banyan tree and the announcer started to shout: 'Vote for the Horse symbol and make your favourite candidate, Raghu Sharma, successful!' over and over. After some time he stopped his shouting, positioned the loudspeaker over a tape-recorder playing film songs and lay down under the banyan tree for a short nap.

The music – which alternated between being inaudible and raucously loud – served only to jar awake the people of Tesri, disturbing their afternoon siesta.

Jagat Ram, who used to work in Kolkata as a mason and had recently come back to the village for the harvest, yelled at the announcer, saying, 'Why don't you reduce the volume? We don't vote for anybody.'

The announcer was astonished. 'What are you *saying*? Are you going to boycott the election over some local issue?'

'No. We are not interested in the elections because we have never been allowed to vote.'

'But, why? Who does not allow you to vote?'

'Our polling booth is in Bhagatpur, but when we go there we are told that our votes have already been cast. So we have simply stopped casting our vote,' Jagat Ram explained.

The announcer had encountered a similar situation before. He knew that very often certain sections of the village were not allowed to vote by the dominant class who captured the booth and voted in lieu of them. 'Fine, I won't make any announcements about the election, but may I continue to play the music for a bit?' the announcer said.

'Yes, of course. There is no harm in that.'

The announcer grinned, shook his head and asked, 'Can I also have some water to drink?'

Jagat Ram asked a young boy to get water for them. The boy came back quickly with a bucket of water and a mug. The announcer and the rickshaw-puller quenched their thirst, rested for a while, and then left – leaving the lingering sound of sweet melodies in the air.

Jagat Ram and his friends sat under the tree and started playing cards. Jamuna Das arrived after a while. Seeing him come towards them they stood up.

'Where did the cycle rickshaw go?' Jamuna Das asked.

'They had come campaigning for the elections. We told them to go away because the people of this village do not vote,' Jagat Ram replied.

Jamuna Das could still hear the song, floating in the air, audible one moment, gone the next. He remembered going to Bhagatpur around ten years ago to cast his vote during one such election. He had stood in the queue at the primary school, which had been designated the polling station. But when he'd reached near the table of the presiding magistrate, the polling agent told him that the vote in the name of Jamuna Das had already been cast. He had protested before the presiding magistrate but to no avail. Subsequently, he had found out that all the votes of his village and Baniya Tola of Bhagatpur had been cast by the people of Bhagatpur in the morning! After that, he had never tried to cast his vote in an election.

He realized that in the changing scenario, and with rising support for the Maoists, people could give their own spin to the manner in which Jagat Ram had asked the announcer to leave the village. As he walked home, the smell of danger in the air assailed his mind with worry.

17.

The election was scheduled just a week later, on the seventh of July. It was also the time when, each year, the monsoons arrived in that part of the country. The Kareh had accumulated some water – ankle- to knee deep – but there was still no swift current in the river. And there were no signs of the pre-monsoon clouds or the easterly wind, pregnant with moisture, either. This was quite unusual. Probably, there had been no rainfall even in the upper reaches of the basin.

Attendance at the evening gathering under the banyan tree was quite large. Everyone from the village was present. The villagers discussed the elections fervently, even though they knew they would not be able to cast their vote. Lakhan Subedar, who by then had become a regular visitor at the gathering, was also present.

'How was the election campaign in Bhagatpur?' Jamuna Das asked Lakhan Subedar.

'I don't really know as I hardly go to Choudhary Tola these days, but the election campaign was not at such a high pitch because there was no candidate from the village,' Lakhan Subedar said.

Jamuna Das remembered that, back when he used to work on Achal Singh's farm, the election had always been a big event. Scores of people parked themselves in Achal Singh's courtyard. They would eat and sleep there and accompany Achal Singh when he went to campaign in other villages. Elaborate makeshift kitchens were set up in the open wherever they went – as if a great picnic were being organized. Achal Singh Mukhia, pink and tall, resplendent in his spotless white kurta-pyjama, with a stole bearing the emblem of the party draped around his shoulders, would supervise everything. Jamuna Das was given the additional responsibility of managing the kitchen and cleaning the veranda.

'How is Achal Singh Mukhia? Is he not active in the election this year?' he inquired.

'He is active as far as the village is concerned. Of the two groups in the village, one led by Achal Singh and the other by Pratap Singh, the first one is stronger,' Lakhan Subedar said.

'We have nothing to do with the election as such. Neither Achal Singh nor Pratap Singh will allow us to cast our votes.'

'We should try to cast our votes this time. If we are stopped, we would go to the authorities.'

'We've tried earlier and failed. Who will listen to poor people like us?'

Suddenly they saw Chowkidar Chedi Paswan wending his way towards them. His beard was uneven, with more hair on his right cheek, which appeared swollen. After coming up to the platform under the tree, Chedi stopped for a moment, looked at the people sitting around and then slowly lowered himself onto the platform. He put down his bag, took off his turban and sighed deeply.

'What happened to you?' Jamuna Das inquired looking at his swollen right cheek.

'I have been suffering from this godforsaken toothache for the last week and there is no doctor around here who can pull it out. Because of the election, I cannot take leave to go to a dentist in town. And I am sick of taking Murli Compounder's pills,' Chedi Paswan said, the agony apparent in his voice.

Everybody looked at him in alarm. It was as if they thought Chedi Paswan was personally responsible for organizing the elections and, because of his aching tooth, the election might not be held.

Then Lakhan Subedar said, 'Why don't you take a day's leave? The elections will not stop because of your absence.'

Chedi Paswan looked at him in disbelief and then winced as he felt a fresh stab of pain. He remembered how the officer in charge of the police station had abused him and threatened that he would be discharged if he went on leave.

'No leave is possible till the election is over, unless I die. This year, the election is going to be full of violence. The Maoists have given a call to boycott the election, which means they will try to stop it by force. Even the landlords are scared. A large police force is coming to man the booth and patrol the area,' Chedi Paswan said.

'What are you supposed to do?' Jamuna Das asked.

'I am responsible for escorting them to various villages because they do not know the area. I also have to arrange food for them and a place to stay in each of the villages.'

The villagers sitting there could not comprehend the magnitude of the election arrangements, or the role of Chedi Paswan who was one of the lowest government functionaries. All they knew was that the chowkidar was the police's representative in their village and in case of any problem they were to contact him. But they were also wary of Chedi Paswan because he was loyal to Achal Singh Mukhia, whom nobody in Tesri trusted.

'With such a large force at its command, why doesn't your police station ensure that the people of Tesri are able to cast their vote?' Lakhan Subedar asked.

The chowkidar, obviously, had no answer and started looking at the branches of the tree overhead. In the flickering light of the lantern, only a few thick branches were visible. It occurred to him then that he himself had not voted in all the sixty years of his life and had not thought even once about his voting rights. 'It is difficult for the people of Tesri to vote when the polling booth for Tesri is located in the primary school at Bhagatpur. We should have a polling booth in our village but we do not have any school or any government building where the booth can be made,' Chedi Paswan finally said.

'If the government wants, it can do anything.'

'Yes, it certainly can. But who will go and meet the authorities and tell them about our problems? Achal Singh Mukhia will not do so as it would be against his interests.'

Jamuna Das was surprised to hear Chedi Paswan's opinion on the issue to ensure voting rights for his villagers. He had never thought about it this way and discussing the issue with anyone other than the villagers, even with Achal Singh Mukhia, was impossible for him. He thought Lakhan Subedar might be able to help but he was not sure why Lakhan Subedar wanted to take on Achal Singh. As always, when he could not find a solution to a problem, he left it to fate.

Jamuna Das said, 'It is news time. We should listen to the news.'

The person sitting next to Jamuna Das switched on the radio. The news was almost over. The newsreader was reading the last headline: 'The administration has made all arrangements for ensuring that the polls take place peacefully, particularly in light of the boycott call given by the Maoists. It will be ensured that every citizen can cast his vote without fear.'

An agriculture bulletin followed the announcement: 'Today we will talk about the diseases of maize...'

Chowkidar Chedi Paswan stood up abruptly, put his turban in his blue bag and said, 'Time to go. There are more important issues to deal with tomorrow than taking care of maize.'

After that everyone started leaving the place one by one. Jamuna Das switched off the radio and picked it up.

While leaving, Lakhan Subedar asked Jamuna Das in a low voice, 'Should we do something for our voting rights?'

'I don't think so. We have to live here even after the elections. We are at the mercy of the landlords of Bhagatpur.'

Lakhan Subedar didn't say anything and went home by the shortcut along the canal.

18.

Just a day before the elections, when the campaigning had ended and the blaring of loudspeakers singing praises of the candidates could no longer be heard, Lakhan Subedar had sat in his courtyard, totally disinterested in the goings-on.

After dinner he took a walk in front of his house – the only habit from his army days that he kept up after his retirement. It was a dark night and innumerable stars shone in the sky. The whole village was quiet, as if it had fallen asleep. Even Choudhary Tola was inordinately quiet. Probably everybody was peacefully asleep in anticipation of a clear win for their candidate.

As he strolled along, Lakhan Subedar's mind went back to his memories of elections during his army days. He had had the option of sending his ballot-papers by post, though he had never managed to actually do so.

This had been his first election after his return to the village. But he had never realized that the people of his mohalla – some of them as well-off as the landowners of Choudhary Tola – were not allowed to cast their votes. He thought nobody would dare stop him from voting if he decided to go, but he knew the consequences. He did not want a head-on confrontation with Achal Singh Mukhia and he also knew that everybody in Choudhary Tola would be united on this issue. He had been lost in these thoughts when, suddenly, he had seen three people standing in front of him. They had come in so stealthily that he did not see where they came from. Lakhan Subedar had been scared. He had heard of the movement of criminals on election-eve to influence the outcome.

'Who are you and what do you want?' he had asked them.

'Calm down, please. We are not your enemies, we won't harm you,' one of them said. 'We are Maoists from across the Kareh. We want to help you to exercise your voting rights because we know that the landowners of this village will not allow it. They capture the polling booth and cast votes in place of the poor and backward people of your mohalla and Tesri.'

Lakhan Subedar was speechless. Only a moment ago, he had been thinking that he would not fight Achal Singh Mukhia and his group even if he was not allowed to cast his vote.

'How can you ensure that?' Lakhan Subedar enquired.

'Leave that to us. Our man will wait near the bridge on the canal. At two in the afternoon, you will have to inform him if anyone from your village or Tesri has been sent back from the polling booth without casting his vote. Then we will take action according to our plan. Do not worry, your name will not be disclosed.'

Lakhan Subedar was in a quandary. He did not understand what action they would take. As such, he had no idea how the Maoists functioned. He did not know how to react. He wanted time to think, but the man had said, 'We will wait for the information tomorrow afternoon at around two,' and then all three vanished into the dark night.

Later Lakhan Subedar had pondered over the issue for a long time. He was not sure whether he should meet them at the bridge at the specified time. He was also not certain that he should send anyone from his mohalla or from Tesri to the polling booth to test whether he was being allowed to vote. The more he thought of it, the more confused he had become.

⌘

The meeting with the three strangers forced him to think about the election and the sad reality that his people were not allowed to cast their vote. Not very long ago, he had been a member of the Indian army. He wondered why the Maoists had picked him. Why did they think it right to contact him for this purpose? Did they know of his encounter with Achal Singh Mukhia? Or had they come to him because he had spent a night at Pratap Singh's hotel? Was it because he went to Tesri almost every day to sit with the villagers under the banyan tree? He was not sure.

Generally Lakhan preferred sleeping in the veranda, where his father, his cousins and other male relatives used to sleep. His bedroom was connected to it by a narrow passage. Outside, on the other side of the bedroom, was a lawn where his wife had planted jasmine flowers. After sitting for a long time in the veranda, he went inside to sleep in his room. His wife was surprised to see him.

'Why have you come here to sleep tonight?' she asked.

'Tomorrow is election day and there will be a lot of movement of people through the night. It is better if I stay inside,' he said, not telling her the real reason for his restlessness.

'But what does that have to do with us?'

'It excites the dogs and I can't sleep when the dogs start barking,' he said, trying to sound casual.

Before going to bed he took out his licensed gun from the almirah, dusted its cover and inspected its barrel. It was a twelve-bore double-barrel gun. He had bought it when he was posted in a peace station where his Commanding Officer, who had good relations with the civil authority, had got him a gun licence. He had always taken his weapon with him wherever he was posted, and had brought it to the village when he retired. He had never shown it to anybody. Nobody in the village knew that he owned a licensed firearm.He cleaned the barrel in the lamplight, took out the plastic pouch that contained the cartridges, stood the gun against the wall in a corner of the room, and put the pouch with the cartridges under his pillow, wanting to be ready for any eventuality. After that he lay down on his bed thinking about the plan for the next day and how he could get information about the situation at the polling booth in Bhagatpur. Without realizing it, he fell asleep even though the dogs were barking as if a thousand thieves had broken into the village.

⌘

The next morning was windy. The easterly wind had increased the humidity, but there was still no sign of clouds. Lakhan Subedar got up and came out to the veranda to stretch. He felt as if he had not slept a wink. His father was walking in front of the veranda. It was quite early in the morning and the eastern horizon had just started turning crimson. Lakhan was familiar with his father's habit of rising early and going to the temple.

Having seen him sitting on the veranda, his father stopped and asked, 'You got up very early today. You could not sleep or what?'

'No. I went to sleep early and got up early,' he lied.

'Today is election day. There may be disturbances at the polling booth. You had better stay home,' his father suggested.

Lakhan thought back to the night. He anticipated disturbances in Bhagatpur but he was not sure whether he should follow the directions of the Maoists and let them know that the people of Tesri or Dhobi Tola had not been allowed to vote. He thought that the Maoists would have other informants as well. He decided that he would not go to cast his vote.

'Is anybody from our mohalla going to vote?' he asked his father.

'No. We don't go. We are Telis by caste and we do not want conflict with anybody. People from Dhobi Tola also don't go because their votes are polled by the youths of Bhagatpur.'

That was when Lakhan had decided how he would spend his day.

He started for the haat at ten in the morning. The sun beat down on him. The humidity was unbearable. Lakhan Subedar wiped his brow and looked at his watch. He would reach Israfil Mian's teashop by ten-thirty if he took the longer route, avoiding Bhagatpur. He would wait at the teashop for news about the polling station in Bhagatpur and then decide his course of action.

The haat was not deserted that day, even though it was not Sunday. Israfil Mian's teashop was doing brisk business. Four police constables sat on the charpoy in front of it. A ramshackle police patrol-jeep was parked there too, with its engine running. Besides the four policemen, three other customers sat inside the teashop and chatted with Israfil Mian who sat on a bench near the hearth. Seeing the police patrol party, Lakhan Subedar went straight inside the shop, wished Israfil Mian, and sat down on the bench where the three customers were seated.

'The shops are supposed to remain closed on election day. How is it that your shop is open?' he asked Israfil Mian.

'The police patrol parties need tea and refreshments while they are on duty,' Israfil Mian grinned.

Lakhan Subedar looked at the policemen sitting outside. They had left their rifles on the charpoy and were sipping tea leisurely, as if there was little threat to them. After a while the driver of the police jeep went and sat in the driver's seat and started to rev the engine.

He shouted, 'Please hurry up. The jeep has only twenty litres of fuel. If I keep the engine running all the while, I doubt we will even make it to the main road.'

One constable guffawed loudly, 'If there is no fuel, switch off the engine and let us stay here. We will go back in the evening.'

All the policemen laughed and went up to the vehicle. The driver pressed down on the accelerator, took a sharp turn and swerved the vehicle in the direction of Dumri.

'The way in which the influence of the Maoists is increasing, the police may not be able to come here as casually as they do now,' Israfil Mian said, watching them leave.

'They have already crossed the Kareh. It is just a matter of time before they control this area as well and set up their parallel government,' one of the customers sitting on the charpoy opined.

Lakhan Subedar listened silently. He was waiting for someone to talk about the polling in Bhagatpur. He realized that the discussion at the teashop was mainly about the Maoists, whom some derided and others praised as the saviours of the people. The teashop was the one place where he could get information not just about Bhagatpur but of surrounding villages as well, because, even on election day, people from different villages dropped in for a bracing cup of chai.

At a quarter past twelve, Jamuna Das arrived at the teashop. 'Jagat Ram had gone to vote in Bhagatpur but he was not allowed to. He was told that his vote had already been cast. No polling agent raised an objection, not even the presiding magistrate. When he insisted on his voting rights, he was threatened and forced to leave,' he told him on an aside.

Lakhan Subedar was sure that Jagat Ram had gone to vote on the direction of the Maoists. He was certain that the Maoists would act now. 'Does Jagat Ram go to vote in each election?' he asked.

'People from Tesri never go to cast their vote because they are threatened and ridiculed and told that their votes have already been polled. I can't understand why Jagat Ram went to vote knowing fully well that he would not be allowed,' Jamuna Das said.

Lakhan Subedar was sure that there would be trouble soon. He did not want to share his apprehensions with Jamuna Das because he thought that Jamuna Das would take him to be a part of the conspiracy.

He excused himself and left, thinking it would be best to remain at home when the crisis broke.

19.

It was around two-thirty in the afternoon.

Polling at the dilapidated school building was almost over. The presiding magistrate, the lone constable and Chowkidar Chedi Paswan were all dozing in the presence of three compliant polling agents who had conspired not to complain against each other in case anyone of them was charged with allowing forged or bogus voting.

Suddenly, gunshots were heard from the periphery of the village. People rushed to take cover even in the village centre. There was panic all around. Nobody knew who was shooting whom. The presiding magistrate ran into the room – not to protect the ballot boxes which were kept there, but to save his own life. The constable followed right behind. Only Chowkidar Chedi Paswan showed some courage and, within seconds of the shooting, dragged his wasted body to the veranda of the Mukhia, knowing it would be the centre of activity in such an emergency.

News spread rapidly about a group of people armed with lethal weapons who had come to the outskirts of the village and opened random fire, killing a woman who was drying clothes on the rooftop, a poor peasant's goat, which was ambling on a six-foot-high boundary wall, and injuring a boy who was playing in front of his house.

It was an attack on the villagers of Bhagatpur, with no specific target.

It was the first attack ever on such a prominent village within a ten-mile radius.

After opening fire, the attackers had gone back towards the Kareh, along the canal – which was presumably the way they had come. As they left, they had strewn pamphlets on which, written in bold black ink, was: 'Achal Singh Mukhia, beware! Your atrocities will not last long… Restore the rights of the poor!' The killers had also shouted slogans as they'd left. They were quite fearless. The people of Bhagatpur also reported spotting another group of equal strength standing by at the outskirts of the village, in case reinforcements were necessary.

When the attackers had gone, people gathered to see what had happened. They saw the woman's dead body; they saw the boy whose left leg was blown to pieces. They didn't really look at the goat, which had died instantly.

Someone in the crowd shouted, 'Call Murli Compounder!' since he was the closest they had to a doctor in the village. Immediately, somebody started on a bicycle to call Murli from Tesri, unmindful of the attackers who could not have gone too far.

⌘

Visibly pale and shaken, Achal Singh Mukhia stood in the crowd, directing people what to do. The villagers lifted the wounded boy onto a charpoy and wound a piece of cloth on his leg. The boy was unconscious. The villagers were scared. Chowkidar Chedi Paswan forgot all about his toothache and his asthma. He saw the pamphlets strewn here and there, and understood their significance even though he was unable to read a single word. He collected the pamphlets and put them in his blue cloth bag to hand over to the in-charge of the police station.

News of the shoot-out spread to the haat. A police patrol-party was already present there and came running to the village. By now everybody had gathered on Achal Singh Mukhia's veranda, where they had taken the injured boy, and were waiting for Murli Compounder. All the people were very agitated. They had never expected such a daring attack on their village in broad daylight. Achal Singh Mukhia was not sitting on his usual reclining chair, but on a wooden cot, leaning against the wall, as if the incident had permanently altered him. He was quiet and grim. All around him people were talking in whispers, as if at a funeral. The boy didn't move. There was no way to quickly get him to a hospital. A grey cloud covered the sky and the humidity increased.

The police patrol party and Murli Compounder arrived at the same time. Murli Compounder looked at the boy in disbelief. He had never seen a leg injured so severely. He opened his plastic bag and pulled out his stethoscope. He put the stethoscope to the boy's chest and realized that he was still alive. He examined the wounded leg carefully and said, 'This is beyond my capability. The child is bleeding profusely. If he is not taken to the doctor in town, he will die from loss of blood.' The police officer, dressed in shabby uniform, looked as tense as the rest of them.

It was decided they would take the boy to town in the police jeep because that was the fastest means of transport available. They put the cot on which the injured boy lay, into the jeep. Two middle-aged men, probably the injured boy's relatives, huddled beside him inside the vehicle. A constable who knew the way to the hospital climbed in next to the driver. Achal Singh Mukhia directed Murli Compounder to accompany them because he thought they might need his assistance on the way.

⌘

Late in the evening, when it was almost dark and the birds had come back to the branches of the tree, three vehicles loaded with police personnel arrived in the village. The people were still gathered in Achal Singh Mukhia's veranda. They were silent, waiting. Then the police officer broke the silence.

'Who is the village head?' he asked.

Everybody turned to look at Achal Singh Mukhia. The officer understood. He addressed Achal Singh: 'We can't discuss such important things in the presence of such a large gathering.'

In any other situation, Mukhia would have refused to talk to the police without the crowd that had gathered in his support. But that day he realized he could no longer afford to annoy the police. He also knew that, from that moment on, his survival in the village would be difficult without their help.

His lips trembled for a moment before he addressed the crowd. 'We are at the mercy of the government. If the police give us security, we will be able to protect our land, our property and our respect. And for that we have to cooperate with the police. Everyone is requested to go back to their homes. Let us do what is best for the people of this village.'

On hearing Mukhia's speech, the crowd started to disperse. After the people left, the police officer spoke to the mukhia and some other influential people from the village about their understanding of the incident. Then he went to inspect the body of the woman who had been killed and the sites where the firing had taken place.

The woman lay with her eyes open. The pool of blood under her back had thickened. She held a piece of cloth tightly in her closed fist. Her face was serene, as if she had died without struggle.

Next, the police officer went to the spot where the dead goat lay. He examined the place thoroughly and found blood marks all along the wall.

'It was ambling along the boundary wall but after the bullet hit, it fell like a bird, squirting its blood on the wall,' Mukhia said.

The police officer did not reply. He was using the torch to examine the dead body of the goat and verify the direction from which the bullet had come.

'Only the innocent die in such conflicts,' he finally said.

By the time the police had finished its forensic work it was very late. They lifted the dead body of the woman, placed it on a cot and brought it to Achal Singh Mukhia's village.

'The postmortem will only be performed tomorrow morning so we will take the dead body to town in the morning,' the police officer said.

Mukhia led the police officer and three of his colleagues inside his room and closed the door. The other constables and armed guards remained outside, in the veranda. The policemen all seated themselves on the chairs kept along the wall.

Then Mukhia went back outside. A few elderly people – campaigners who camped there – were still present. He told them, 'The police party will sleep here tonight. You can all sleep in that shed.' He pointed to a shed on the other side of the ground where he stored his cattlefeed.

Going back to his room the mukhia called for his servant and asked him to get some glasses and water. He then opened his cabinet, pulled out a bottle of rum and put it on the table. 'Please have a drink till the food gets ready,' he said.

The policemen all had their drinks in Achal Singh's room. His servants plied them with plates of fried fish and vegetable salad. Mukhia personally refilled their glasses. When the police were so sloshed that they were unable to carry themselves, he asked the servant to serve dinner. They were so inebriated, they hardly ate.

While they were eating one of the villagers who had gone with the injured boy to town, came running to the veranda and knocked at the Mukhia's door. Achal Singh Mukhia saw him and indicated that he should wait outside. When Achal Singh went out the villager informed him that the boy was dead. 'He died when we reached Dumri Chowk. The police have taken the dead body to keep in the mortuary. They have asked us to come tomorrow morning for the postmortem.'

Achal Singh received the news in silence.

After dinner the three police officers slept in the room attached to the veranda, drunk on the rum that Mukhia kept especially for august guests like them.

⌘

Around midnight, when the officers were fast asleep and the constables had nodded off with their rifles under their heads, three young men from the village came to call on Achal Singh Mukhia. They took him to the house of another influential man of the village called Ajit Singh. At Ajit Singh's house ten or twelve men waited in the veranda hunched around a lamp without a glass cover, talking in low, conspiratorial tones.

'We have to take revenge. It is not an attack on an individual. It is an attack on the prestige of the village,' one of them said to Achal Singh when he joined them.

'But we can't get the actual attackers so easily.'

Just then an owl hooted, inauspiciously. And at that evil hour, the villagers decided that they would take revenge by attacking Dhobi Tola before dawn. They knew that they would be able to do so easily; they expected no resistance because Dhobi Tola was a small, poor hamlet of lowcastes, mainly involved in menial work like washing and cleaning the landlords' houses in Bhagatpur.

None in that select gathering objected to the decision, not even Achal Singh Mukhia.

So in the dead of night, seven strong men with their faces covered, armed with swords and spears, and almost as drunk as the police officers lying passed out in Mukhia's room, encircled Dhobi Tola and blocked all exit points. Then another group of equal strength went inside the hutments to pick out all the young, able-bodied men of the basti. They were surprised to find none. The absence of the men strengthened the suspicion of their involvement in the attack on Bhagatpur.

The men then pulled out three women, two boys of about fifteen or sixteen and an old man, and forcibly took all six to the bamboo grove alongside the canal by the other end of the village. There they hacked them one by one, and threw their dismembered bodies into the canal.

Having done their deed the young men came back to see the Mukhia. He sat in his veranda on his armchair, amidst the police officers sleeping on, obliviously, their rifles under their heads. The men wanted to share the details of their mission with the mukhia but he simply nodded his acknowledgement and sent them on their way.

The police officers did not stir. Chowkidar Chedi Paswan lay in a corner of the veranda too, coughing intermittently.

When they woke up in the morning they found the village enveloped in an ominous quiet.

20.

The menfolk of Tesri sat under the banyan tree, in the early hours of the morning, continuing their discussion of the Maoist attack that had occurred at Bhagatpur the previous day.

The men who had run away from Dhobi Tola immediately after the incident and had taken shelter in Tesri – fearing a reprisal from the folks in Choudhary Tola – had left for home a few hours earlier. They had come to Tesri to spend the night because they had anticipated being attacked by the people of Bhagatpur in retaliation, even though they had no role in the incident. They had also feared that they would be arrested and taken to the police station for interrogation. Women, children, the aged and the infirm had been left behind. It was a twenty-minute walk along the canal road, through the mango grove, to Tesri.

When they'd reached Tesri, they had found most of the men of the village under the banyan tree. Speculations were rife: that at least fifteen people had died in the attack; that Achal Singh Mukhia had also died because of the extensive injuries he'd suffered in the firing; that they had only come to kill animals but the bullets had hit the people by mistake. Everyone's imagination was running riot. For once the radio had was switched off, because no news was as important as that of the incident at Bhagatpur.

The people of Tesri had also been worried that those in Bhagatpur might attack them in retaliation. In fact, the youth of the village had readied to counter any such an attack on them and had planned to keep watch all through the night. Their clubs, spears and swords were at the ready.

Seeing the people from Dhobi Tola, Jamuna Das had assumed that they too had come to get some more news about the incident but when they made no move to return to their homes Jamuna Das had realized that they wanted to stay overnight. He did not want to give them protection as that would further damage his relations with Achal Singh Mukhia.

'Why have you people come here?' he asked them outright.

For a long time, they had said nothing. As if there was nothing to say. Then the oldest among them, Bhiku Dhobi, spoke: 'We will stay here tonight for we fear that the police may take us to the police station or the people of Bhagatpur might attack us.'

'What happened, exactly?' Jamuna Das had asked wanting a clear idea about the incident.

'We don't know. We were in our mohalla when we heard gunshots. Later, we came to know that a group of people, probably the Maoists, had attacked the village, fired randomly and left. They were shouting slogans against Mukhia, asking him to end his atrocities against the poor and give voting rights to them. We ran away, fearing that the landlords would target us or tell the police that we had called the Maoists,' Bhiku Dhobi said.

Jamuna Das had been in a dilemma. Should he give them shelter in the village or not? But then, Bhagat Ram, excited by all the talk, had said, 'Stay wherever you feel like and share food with us.' Bhagat Ram had always been vocal against the people of Bhagatpur and, by and by, the youth of the village had started to look upon Bhagat Ram as their leader.

The people from Dhobi Tola declined to eat. They said that they would go back early in the morning as the greatest danger was during the night. So Bhagat Ram asked one of the boys to fetch the bucket of water and the mug that they kept under the tree, in case one of them needed a drink in the night, and then the men of Tesri had gone home. The men of Dhobi Tola had lain down under the banyan, their thoughts with the women, the children and the aged they had left behind.

Early in the morning, when the eastern horizon had not even turned grey and the roosters were busy crowing, Bhiku Dhobi had woken up with a start to find Champa Devi standing there with half a dozen people from Dhobi Tola. She looked tired and troubled, as if she had not slept for many days.

'They came in the night and took our people,' she said to him, tears rolling down her cheeks.

The other people sleeping there got up too. She was crying loudly now and becoming hysterical. 'They were so many, and their faces were covered. They forced all of us to get out of our houses and then they selected six people and took them away. Nobody knows where they are.'

Hearing her cries, the villagers of Tesri had woken up too. Everyone gathered around and tried to console her. Then all the men from Dhobi Tola abruptly left for their homes to find out if one of their relatives was among those who had been taken away. The village became quiet again and everyone stayed under the banyan tree all day. They talked about the incident at Bhagatpur incessantly, and nobody went to the haat for fear of the police.

Around eight in the morning, when the children of Tesri were swimming and fishing in the canal, they spotted some clothes floating on the water. They swam in to grab the clothes thinking they would use them to trap fish. But when they got closer they saw that the pieces of clothes had shapes and figures, and then they realized that there were dead bodies afloat in the canal. They screamed and shouted. They jumped out of the canal and ran to the banyan tree where everybody was still idling.

'There are dead bodies in the canal! We did not count them, but there are many! Some women, some men!' they shouted.

'Where in the canal?' Jamuna Das asked not wanting to believe them.

'Where we swim everyday and catch fish.'

Everybody ran towards the canal. Some of the boys were still waiting by the bank. The first corpse they saw was the body of a woman whose face was covered and one arm was missing. There were deep gashes in her stomach, as if it had been pierced by spears. Then they spotted another body. It was a boy of around fifteen. His face had been smashed. They panicked when someone recognized the boy. They knew his name. It was Bhiku Dhobi's grandson, Suresh. After some time, more dead bodies floated upstream. A few of the men got into the canal and pulled the bodies to the bank. There were six bodies in all, all hacked, all missing a limb or two.

Then, Chowkidar Chedi Paswan arrived at the scene and was utterly aghast. His breathing became loud and erratic. His knees buckled and he fell to the ground. 'God alone knows who has done this despite the presence of so many policemen in the village. I am going to have a tough time ahead,' he said.

The people gathered around him, all talking at once about how they thought the killings might have taken place and who might have been involved. After some time, Chowkidar regained his poise and said, 'It is the first such incident that has happened in this area, but I don't think it's the last.'

'God alone knows that,' Jamuna Das said.

'Please go and inform the police officer who is camping in Achal Singh Mukhia's house,' Chowkidar said.

'I don't feel like going to that village in such a situation,' Jamuna Das replied.

By that time, the news of the bodies floating in the canal had spread everywhere.

A short while later they saw the police officer coming towards them along with a posse of armed men, followed by a large number of people from Dhobi Tola. Men and women were running down to the river and when they reached the banks where the dead bodies lay, the whole crowd set up a wail of lamentation. Almost all the women were screaming. 'Oh, God! They have killed women and children.' Everybody wanted to see the dead bodies, to see the extent of the injuries inflicted; to see how much they were made to suffer before they died. That was when the police officer commanded them to stand back and Chowkidar brandished his staff. 'Everyone! Stand away from the dead bodies,' he wheezed.

The constables formed a circle around the dead bodies to stop the people from getting closer. The women from Dhobi Tola sat at a distance from where they could watch the goings-on without disturbing them.

Seeing the dead bodies on the bank of the canal, even the Sub-Inspector grew nervous. He took a piece of paper from his pocket, wrote a message on it and called Chedi Paswan. 'Go and deliver this message to the wireless operator who is sitting in the mukhia's veranda.'

Chowkidar ran as fast as he could with his one bad leg and wooden staff.

By evening everyone of importance and consequence in the district had descended on Bhagatpur. But nobody could find Achal Singh Mukhia because he had fled by then and no one knew where he was.

21.

At midnight there was a knock on Murli Compounder's door. After the recent killings in Dhobi Tola, Murli was afraid to open his door at night and was reluctant to attend to patients at that hour. He lay in bed and hoped that whoever it was would go away after knocking a few times, but the knocking persisted and its intensity increased. He realized that he would have to get up and attend to the patient.

It was a full-moon night and visibility was excellent. Despite this, he picked up the torch that he habitually kept next to his pillow and looked at his watch. It was twelve-fifteen. A pleasant September night breeze was blowing.

He went to the door, 'Who is it?' he asked.

'There is a patient, it is an emergency,' someone replied.

Murli could recognize the voice of everyone from his village even in his sleep and knew that the man outside was not from Tesri. He also doubted that the person was from Bhagatpur because, in that case, he would have called Murli by name and identified himself. Now Murli Compounder was a bit scared.

He asked again, 'Who are you? From which village?'

'Ibrahimpur. It is an emergency.'

'Where is the patient? Have you brought him along with you?'

'Yes. The patient is also coming. I came ahead so that you could get ready.'

Murli Compounder opened the door and saw two men standing outside. One of them was in a shirt and a pyjama, the other in a dhoti and kurta. Both of them had thin cotton gamchas wrapped around their necks. In the bright moonlight their features were sharply visible. Murli Compounder tried to remember if he had seen them before, but he could not place them.

'Will the patient come here or have you come to take me along with you?'

'He will be reaching here soon,' one of them said.

Murli Compounder asked the men to wait. He went back inside and returned with a lantern and the key to the clinic. Everyone in his house remained asleep because a patient knocking in the middle of the night was not unusual.

Once he unlocked the clinic both the men followed him inside and sat on the bench opposite the doctor's table. Murli Compounder set the lantern down and its light cast a surreal look on the room. The occasional bark of a dog was heard from outside. Apart from that it was so quiet that Murli Compounder could hear his own heart beating.

'Why didn't you bring the patient in the day?' Murli asked.

'We could not have moved during the day and we can't go to the government hospital. That is why we are here.'

'Why?' Murli was confused.

'The patient is the Area Commander of the Maoist group. He has been hurt in police firing. If we go to a government hospital, the doctor there will inform the police.'

Murli understood their predicament and their reason for choosing to come to him. There was not a single qualified doctor within a radius of ten miles, and the police were only three miles away, in Dumri Chowk. Murli had treated several cases that should have had police intervention before this, but none of those cases had ever been connected to the Maoists. He was scared of the possible consequences of handling this case. If they found out that he had treated the injured Maoist leader the police were sure to question him. They might even arrest him for harbouring and aiding the Maoists.

He looked at the two men sitting opposite him. They were reserved and subdued and looked nothing like the dreaded Maoists he had imagined, about whom he had heard so many fearsome stories. But he had also heard about their ways, and he knew that if he did not attend to the patient they might forcibly take him to their camp, deep inside the jungle.

Suddenly, hearing footsteps outside, the two men sprang to attention. One of them peered outside the window and on recognizing the people outside, relaxed visibly. 'They have come,' he told his partner and both of them went outside to receive them. A minute later all of them were inside the clinic. Now there were five of them. The three new visitors were draped in shawls. Murli was sure they were weapons concealed beneath them.

'Who is the patient?' he asked.

One of the men removed his shawl. His left arm had a sling with a dirty bandage wrapped around it. Murli switched on his torch and looked closely at the arm. The bandage was soiled with congealed blood and the foul smell of a festering wound emanated from it. Murli was surprised that there was no sign of pain on the patient's face.

'Please sit down,' he said.

The patient sat on a bench spread with a plastic sheet, and then lay down. Murli undid the hook of the sling and started slowly undoing the bandage. The patient clenched his teeth.

'How did this happen?'

'A bullet went through my arm, grazing the bone.'

Murli examined the wound. It was deep and the muscle was badly ruptured. It had become infected from lack of care. Pus had formed inside. It had not even been stitched. Without an X-ray, he could not ascertain whether the bone had been damaged. He cleansed the area around the wound and then filled it with antiseptic. The patient had a tremendous capacity to bear pain – in proper hospitals, doctors performed such procedures only after using a local anaesthetic. The patient did not even wince.

While Murli dressed the wound, two of the men stood outside, keeping watch. Of the other two, one assisted Murli by holding down the patient while the other held the torch. Murli finished his work quickly and efficiently and then went outside to wash his hands. When he returned, the three men, including the patient, were sitting on the bench.

'How much is your fee?' the man who had been holding the patient asked.

Murli Compounder thought for a moment. It was risky to take money from them. After all, they were the dreaded Maoists who fought against the might of the state. Nobody could survive in the remote areas without their consent. He thought it best to benefit from their acquaintance. If they trusted him he could move freely about in the area without any fear. 'There will not be any charge for this,' he said.

'You have to take money from us,' the patient insisted.

'You people are in trouble and are fighting for a cause. Allow me to at least contribute this much,' Murli said.

The men exchanged glances. Murli opened his plastic bag and took out some tablets. He held out two strips of medicine, covered in colourful plastic.

'Take both the tablets three times a day for the next five days. Hopefully the wound will heal within fifteen days,' Murli said to the wounded man.

'When do I have to come again?'

'Preferably after three days. You have to change the dressing within a week.'

The men left by the canal road. They moved out so quietly that even the dogs didn't bark. As he watched them go, Murli assumed that they would cross the Kareh at night and then go to any of the villages across the river – all of which were all part of their bastion. He was not sure if they were actually from Ibrahimpur or if they had given him a false address.

Once they had left Murli tried to go back to sleep but his mind was troubled with too many thoughts. He knew that they would come back again. He also knew that now his reputation as a doctor would spread far and wide amongst the Maoists. They were sure to come to him for all kinds of treatment and no doubt they would also take him to the jungle to examine patients.

He had to discuss this situation with somebody. Suddenly he thought of his mentor Sundaram from Arogyadham in Dhanwar.

He only fell asleep in the wee hours of morning, when the moonlight had begun to lose its sheen.

⌘

By now it had become a very familiar route: from his village to Dumri Chowk and from there to the Puraini Railway Station, then to Ismailpur by train and to Dhanwar on foot. He knew the way like he knew the back of his hand because he had traversed it so many times... But this visit was different. He was in trouble and wanted to seek Sundaram's advice.

By the time Murli reached Dhanwar the sun's rays had become slanted. He had come by the same train that had left stranded him two miles ahead of Ismailpur more than fifteen years ago. He arrived at the main gate of Arogyadham exactly at six-thirty because the train was late. The hospital compound was quite deserted. Had the train been on time, he would have reached at two-thirty. He could have asked Basanti, the kitchen girl, to give him lunch. And when Sundaram came out of his room after his afternoon nap, he could have chatted with him.

Sadly, he found nobody at the main door, not even a stray dog loitering about. The bougainvillea creepers grew thickly over the boundary wall. The main gate was unlocked. Murli Compounder opened it and entered the compound without ringing the bell. He found Sundaram sitting on a rocking chair in the veranda outside his living room reading a newspaper. Many magazines and books lay on the side table. Sundaram was so absorbed in his reading that he didn't notice Murli till he stood right beside him.

'When did you come? I didn't even realize that somebody had entered the compound. Probably age is catching up with me,' Sundaram stood up and shook hands with Murli when he said Namaste.

Murli sat down on a stool and put his jute bag on the floor. He noticed the changes that had come about during the last few months. Three huge tree trunks lay along the wall, being seasoned in the sun. Just a few yards away from Sundaram's room was a small temple that was being renovated. Two carpenters were working on the porch of the temple. A herd of goats entered the campus through a wicket gate. Murli saw Basanti walking towards the veranda with a glass of water on a small tray.

'Why don't you make some pakoras for Murli?' Sundaram asked her.

'I will get some tea and biscuits first,' she said.

'No need to make anything now. Tea and biscuits will be fine. I will have an early dinner,' Murli said.

Basanti went to the pantry again and returned with two cups of tea and a plate of biscuits.

Murli's mind went back to his first few days with Sundaram. He used to eat his meals in the students' hostel that Sundaram ran for poor boys. Once in a while, Sundaram would ask his maid to give him food from the kitchen. This had made Murli feel very privileged. He took out two large bottles of honey from his jute bag and set them on the floor.

'Again you have got honey for me. I will have to find a buyer for your honey because I have still not finished the supply you brought earlier,' Sundaram laughed.

'I guess you haven't been able to go to the city, otherwise you would have gifted it to your friends there.'

'Yes. I have not been to the city in quite a while. The renovation work in the temple keeps me busy here.'

When they finished their tea, Sundaram got up and went towards the porch of the temple where the carpenters were working. Murli also followed him. The carpenters were polishing the wooden board.

'Look at this gate. I am thinking of making it more ornate. You see those tree trunks lying there? That's teak. I bought it from a villager. Once the woodwork is finished, the temple will look great.'

'Yes. The wood looks quite seasoned. The carpenters are doing a good job.'

Sundaram took him for a round of the temple premises, stopping at each point that he had planned to renovate. He explained his plans to Murli in detail and told him exactly how he wanted the work done. Then they walked back to the front again, where they had left their shoes. It was almost dark now. The goats were in their shed. Murli remembered, even when he worked in Arogyadham hospital, Sundaram had kept a large number of goats. Poor people from neighbouring villages would come to borrow money from Sundaram and he would oblige them, but at the cost of impounding their goat or cow. Usually, they would take them animals back after repaying the loan, but some of them would not be able to pay back and, by and by, the number of goats in the hospital compound had increased. Sundaram used to say, 'If you don't impound anything in lieu of the loan amount, they have a tendency to take loans and spend the money on liquor.'

'I was reading the newspaper. Your area is disturbed. The Maoists have taken over the entire area and are running a parallel government. There have been frequent encounters with the police. How is your village doing?' Sundaram enquired, sitting on his chair in the veranda.

'Tesri has been partially affected. Some of the boys have gone underground and joined hands with the Maoists.'

'I am told that they have become active in this area too. They are trying to get a foothold and are enticing young boys to join them. But I have not come across them personally and they have not disturbed me so far.'

'Well, I have been disturbed,' Murli said.

'How?' Sundaram was intrigued.

'They know that I am a doctor. The injured Maoists come to me for treatment. They come late at night.'

'So? What is the problem?'

'The police will come to know of this sooner or later. The landlords of Bhagatpur are the sworn enemies of the Maoists. They will tell the police that I am their accomplice. And the Maoists will not like it if I don't treat them.'

Sundaram absorbed this while Basanti came in and lit the kerosene lamp in the veranda. He was lost in thought. In the quietness of the surroundings, the sound of the wind-chime hanging on the main door gave a sense of time.

'Yes, it is a dilemma,' Sundaram finally said.

'What should I do? I have come here to take your advice.'

Sundaram thought again, and after a few minutes he said, 'The problem is not going to be over soon. As I understand the situation, the Maoists are going to rule the remote areas for a long time, or at least till the time the government initiates a sustained drive against them. They have the people's support as well. I suppose your village and Dhanwar come under the same district? I know the police chief of the district and I can take you to him.'

Murli wondered whether meeting the police chief would solve his problem or worsen it. At the very least, he would have to explain to the police chief that he had no option but to treat the Maoists, else they would kill him.

Sundaram got up and said, 'I am going to pray for a while. We will take this honey as a gift for the police chief.'

22.

When Sundaram stopped his old station-wagon by the gate of an old building with high boundary walls, a sprawling garden and lush green trees, Murli realized that they had reached the police chief's residence. Bold letters in brass on a wooden plate said, Alok Saxena. He grew even more apprehensive.

The guard standing at the gate did not ask any questions – they probably knew Sundaram well – and allowed the station-wagon to enter. Sundaram parked his vehicle alongside the other police vehicles parked there. Murli got off the car worrying that the policeman might question his presence and his purpose for being there, but seeing Sundaram walk in so confidently, he followed suit.

There were two rooms with a small veranda near the entrance of the house. One room had a nameplate on its door. Inside the other, three people sat at a table sorting out a sheaf of paper. Seeing Sundaram in the veranda, one of them came out, and wished him. 'Sahib is sitting in the office,' he said and immediately opened the door to the other room.

Sundaram asked Murli to wait outside and went in.

Murli waited in the room where the police chief's assistants were working. All along the wall of the room were wooden racks stacked with hundreds of files. The man who had wished Sundaram asked Murli to take a seat. A rickety fan whirred noisily.

The personal assistant came back after some time and asked Murli, 'Will you have a cup of tea?'

'No thanks,' Murli replied. Working with Sundaram for a long time had taught him some measure of social courtesy.

'Do you live with Sundaram sahib?' the assistant asked.

'No. I live in Tesri, quite far from Sundaram's hospital. But I used to work with him earlier.'

'Oh, that is a dangerous area. Even the police is scared to go there.'

'Yes, but we live quite comfortably there.'

'What is in this packet?'

He did not want to say it was a bottle of honey that he'd got from his village for the police chief. 'Sundaram has brought something for your sahib. I don't know what it is.'

Suddenly a bell rang. The assistant ran towards the police chief's office. Within seconds, he was back. 'Sahib has called you inside,' he said.

The assistant left him at the door. Inside the room Murli saw Sundaram sitting on a chair, chatting with the police chief. It was a very large and well-appointed room. The police chief sat behind a black table, swivelling about in his chair every now and then. After a while, Sundaram asked Murli to sit.

'This is Murli. He lives in Tesri. He used to work in my hospital earlier. He is a trained compounder and works as a pharmacist in Tesri,' he said.

The police chief looked him straight in the eye, as if trying to size him up. 'Sundaram has told me about your problem. You need not worry. The police will not harass you because you are not helping the Maoists willingly. But in case you get any advance information about their movement in the area, please come and tell me. Nobody will find out that you passed on the information to us.'

'But how will I be able to meet you? The guard outside will stop me,' Murli said.

The police chief pressed the call-bell and immediately the assistant came rushing in.

'This is Murli. I am going to give him my visiting card. If he comes here to meet me and shows the card at the gate he should be allowed to come inside, even if it is the middle of the night. Inform everybody about this,' the police chief instructed him.

After the assistant left, the police chief turned back to Murli: 'Don't put your life in danger just to give us information. Come only when it is safe. We will reward you suitably.'

'I make good money in the village and I don't require financial help. I am scared because I cannot refuse the Maoists.'

'Don't worry. We will take care of that.'

There was silence for a while. Sundaram looked at Murli and gestured towards the packet. Murli handed it to Sundaram.

'He has got some honey for you. This is pure honey collected in the village.' Sundaram put the packet on the table and the police chief smiled. Sundaram then asked Murli to wait outside.

Murli left the room still unsure whether meeting the police chief had resolved his problem or made it worse.

Sundaram and Murli left the police chief's residence at a quarter-to-eight and headed back to the main office of Arogyadham, which was in the town, barely fifteen minutes from the police chief's residence. It had a guest-house attached to it. They had decided to stay there overnight because Sundaram did not want to drive back to the village in the dark.

They drove past the crowded main square of the town. The teashop in the square was doing brisk business even though, by Murli's village's standard, it was time to sleep. People sat outside on a bench under a streetlight. There was electricity here. Murli thought how much more advanced the town was than his village.

As they were getting off the car Sundaram said, 'Even if you have the ear of the police chief you still have to be careful with the police.'

23.

It was a hot and humid night. It had rained through the day but the temperature hadn't fallen, in fact, the humidity had become more unbearable. Ramu Hajjam lay on his charpoy after dinner and fanned himself with a hand fan. A lantern in the doorway burnt with its wick lowered to keep the insects away. It was no longer raining now but the sky was still overcast. Not a single star was visible. Ramu Hajjam knew that such nights were always the darkest ones of the year. People in the villages slept very early on such dark nights and one could not hear anything except the sound of the last few raindrops falling on the roof.

As Ramu Hajjam was about to fall into an uneasy slumber, he heard someone push open the wicket gate. He thought perhaps it was a stray dog trying to get in. Phulmani was sleeping inside the room and his mother lay on a rug in the veranda not far from his bed. He looked at them to make sure they were both in bed. On rainy nights like these stray animals searching for a covered shelter often tried to sneak into people's houses. His house didn't have a proper door. The boundary wall around his house had only a waist-high wicket gate. While he was still debating whether to go outside and see who was trying to open the door or go back to sleep, he saw Pawan standing in front of him.

Ramu Hajjam looked closer. Water dripped from his son's forehead. It was probably raining heavily somewhere not far from his house. Three men were with him. They stood in the courtyard looking watchful and alert, as if providing security to Pawan. At that moment it began to rain again, thick and heavy. Ramu Hajjam sat up on his charpoy.

Pawan said, 'I want to see Mother.'

Ramu Hajjam looked wordlessly towards the cot where his wife lay asleep. The next moment, Pawan was inside the room. Phulmani got up on hearing her son's footsteps and screamed with joy. Ramu Hajjam could hear Phulmani crying loudly even in the din of the heavy downpour.

He heard Pawan say, 'Don't cry. I will keep on visiting you. I have taken a pledge to avenge my father's humiliation. I have to restore the respect of the people of this village. I will come back once I have redeemed myself.'

But Phulmani couldn't stop crying. Then Ramu saw Kalavati wake up. She picked up the lantern, raised the wick and moved inside. Soon he heard her crying too: 'Why did you leave us, son? My eyes have turned to stones waiting to see you each day.' Her cries turned into a loud wail.

Kalavati had lifted the lantern up to Pawan's face and Ramu Hajjam caught his first proper glimpse of his son's face in a long time. It was no longer young and boyish. It had become angular and tanned, his cheeks were sunken and his cheek-bones stuck out prominently. Ramu Hajjam felt an overwhelming grief overpower him. He had to sit down. He heard Pawan say, 'I have to go now. I can't stay any longer.'

'Eat something before you go, my son. You have not eaten food cooked by me in such a long time,' Phulmani said.

Pawan hesitated for a moment and then asked for just a bite of anything available and Ramu Hajjam saw Phulmani race towards the veranda and then run back with some food on a plate. He heard her say, 'Eat all you want, my son. Nobody will come here in the dead of night.'

But Pawan didn't stay long. He ate a bite hurriedly, came back to the veranda, went up to his father and touched his feet. This surprised Ramu because Pawan had never touched his feet before. The next moment, he was gone. It was as if he had merged with the dark night or dissolved in the rain.

He heard Phulmani and Kalavati sob loudly. Then Kalavati went back to her rug and lay down muttering some prayers for the safety of her grandson. That was when Ramu Hajjam felt his mind beginning to fog. He started dreaming.

⌘

And in his dream, he saw a great saint with a halo around his head and a shining face reflecting absolute peace and equanimity. The saint sat on a high pedestal adorned with beautiful carvings. A group of people sat on the ground in front of him. Ramu Hajjam saw that he too was there, present in the audience.

The saint was telling the story of a trusted servant of a king who lived in his palace and carried messages for the king to far-off places, leaving behind his young, only son. Once, when he was away, two boys of the royal family strangled his son to death. When he came back and found out what had happened the trusted servant planned his revenge.

A savage tiger leashed by a strong chain was kept in the royal palace. When the two boys of the royal family went to see it, the king's servant thought it an opportune time. He took hold of the boys and threw them at the feet of the tiger. Within moments, the tiger had mauled them to death. And the servant declared, 'Now that my heart's wish has been fulfilled, I will leave this palace. But before I go I will tell the king what I have done.'

And so he went before the king, prostrated before him and said, 'My Lord, your children killed my poor son so I threw them to the savage tiger. Now I must leave as I cannot live here any longer."

The king was righteous. He said, 'You retaliated because you were wronged. And now that you have taken your revenge, your anger will abate. You should stay.'

But the servant said, 'I cannot live here in peace. I must go.'

At that moment, Ramu Hajjam wanted to get up and ask the saint, 'And what about my son? He has gone to avenge my humiliation. When will he come back? And will he be punished once he has accomplished his task? I also suffer in his absence. What should I do?'

But then he saw in his dream that neither the saint nor the people were there. He started running to find them, but total darkness engulfed him and he woke up, drenched in sweat, only to find Kalavati muttering her prayers and the rain falling.

24.

Nothing could stop the evening gathering under the banyan tree in Tesri: not the Maoist attack on Bhagatpur; not the killings in Dhobi Tola; not the rising influence of the Maoists in the area. It was sometimes hindered by the rain and cold, though.

'Last night Pawan came home to meet his mother,' one of the men in the gathering whispered.

'Yes, I heard he came when it was raining heavily so nobody could hear anything. Earlier in the morning, the police had come from the haat searching for Pawan,' Israfil Mian said.

It was the middle of August, the peak of the rainy season. There had been no evening gathering for the last two days because it had been raining continuously. The Kareh was full to the brim and flowing with tremendous speed. Nobody dared even lower their feet in its waters. Pawan's unannounced visit at this time shocked everybody because it meant that he and his Maoist friends had been camping on their side of the river. The villagers were also surprised that the police had got wind of his presence.

'How did the police know that Pawan was here at night? There would have been a great commotion if both of them were here at the same time,' Bhagat Ram said.

They all fell silent imagining the situation. The Maoists and the police would have opened fire right there in the village.

'Someone in the village is a police informant,' Lakhan Subedar said. He had come to Tesri at four in the afternoon that day, braving the rains with an umbrella. Before starting from his home in Bhagatpur he had looked up at the sky many times, pondered its colour. He had eventually decided that he would go to Tesri even though the dark clouds clearly meant torrential rain.

Everyone turned to look at Chowkidar Chedi Paswan who was sitting among them with his head bowed, as if he were dozing. Earlier, the needle of suspicion would have automatically pointed at him, but now the villagers knew that Chedi Paswan had changed his loyalties. He was officially the government's representative in the village but, after the killings at Dhobi Tola, his heart was firmly with the people of his own village.

'Someone in the village is definitely a police informant, otherwise the police had no reason to come to the village on such a dark, rainy night,' Israfil Mian said.

For the villagers it was a serious issue that needed to be probed.

'If we find out who the informant is we will tell Pawan and then the Maoists can decide for themselves,' Bhagat Ram said.

Jamuna Das was quiet all through this talk. He thought it was a sensitive issue that should not be discussed openly. He wanted to change the topic. 'Does Achal Singh Mukhia come to the haat?' he asked Israfil Mian.

'He comes once in a while, always with a band of armed men. And he sits in the police tent. He orders tea there itself.'

'How does he look? Has he become very old?'

'No. He looks just as he has for the last ten years.'

Jamuna Das was disturbed by how the relations between the two villages had worsened. The people of Tesri had stopped working in the farms of the landowners of Bhagatpur. Nor had he gone to pay his respects to Achal Singh Mukhia after the incident at Dhobi Tola; he was not sure what Mukhia's reaction would be.

'Now the people of Bhagatpur do not venture out beyond their village. They are even scared of going to their farms without armed protection,' Bhagat Ram said.

'The situation has also changed the equation between the two sworn enemies. Earlier, a large group sided with Pratap Singh. Now the whole village is with Achal Singh Mukhia,' Lakhan Subedar said.

'Yes, the challenge from the Maoists has united

them. Someone told me they have formed an armed group to fight the Maoists,' Jamuna Das said.

Just then they saw Murli Compounder walking towards them. Murli rarely participated in their discussions as he was always too busy. Today he joined the group and sat down on the platform without wishing anybody.

'Murli Compounder can give us the right picture of the situation in Bhagatpur; he goes around everywhere in the area,' Lakhan Subedar said.

Murli Compounder said nothing. He had never bothered with the gossip in the village. He had no time to sit and chat about village politics because he was busy attending to patients. Moreover, he felt that he was on neither side. The landowners of Bhagatpur, the villagers of Tesri and the Maoists were all his patients. He could not afford the enmity of any one of them.

'The situation is not good anywhere. Across the river, tension in the villages is very high. The landowners move with armed bands and the Maoists have their armed squad. The landowners are unable to till their land for fear of the Maoists. The tension between the two has left the land unploughed,' Murli Compounder said.

'This stage was bound to come. How long will the poor suffer the atrocities of the landowners? We have no option but to fight for our rights,' Lakhan Subedar said.

'Now they are also scared of us. Earlier they didn't even treat us as human beings,' Bhagat Ram seconded Lakhan Subedar.

Night insects flew into the flickering light of the lantern. Chowkidar Chedi Paswan fell asleep, sitting where he was. The high humidity predicted more rain.

After a long pause Jamuna Das said, 'Whatever the outcome, the whole conflict has left a bitter memory in everyone's mind.'

It began to rain. Lakhan Subedar looked up at the angry sky. It was going to be a long walk home in the rain. He decided not to unfurl his umbrella because he was going to get drenched anyway.

25.

Seven people sat cross-legged in a circle, strategizing on ways to increase their area of influence. A kerosene lantern in the centre of the room cast its dim light on their faces, the shadows it threw making them look even more haggard and drawn. It was past ten in the night but they were not in any hurry to wind up the meeting and go to sleep. Some of them had walked all day from far-off locations and had arrived only in the evening. They were determined to talk.

The village they had chosen to hold their meeting was so remote and disconnected from the rest of the world that nobody from the local government administration had bothered to stop by in the last three years. Now, after they had taken control, even the village chowkidar had stopped going to the police station to report about the village.

The hut where the people conferred was on the outer periphery of the village, but all the villagers were aware that top-ranking Maoist leaders assembled there frequently to chalk out their strategy.

'We need to augment our presence through the trans-Kareh area. How many full-time cadres do we have in that region?' one of the persons in the group asked. His face was bright, his hair shining black and curly, his voice authoritative.

'For the last year our presence in that area has been up to the village Tesri. Earlier we had only one boy from that village but now we have three boys from that region: two from Tesri and one from Dhobi Tola,' a young man, who was the area commander of trans-Kareh area, replied.

'Since you are the area commander you would know how to motivate people to join our struggle.'

'There is a long history of exploitation in that area. The younger ones from the oppressed communities have started raising their voices against the atrocities committed against them,' the area commander said.

'Does that mean we can get more boys from that area now?'

'One of the three boys from that area shows a lot of promise...'

'Who?'

'Pawan. His father is a barber from Tesri.'

'What assignment has been given to him?'

'He is in our armed squad.'

'Keep him in your team. Since he comes from that area, he will be able to motivate other young people from there to join our ranks.'

After the discussion about the trans-Kareh area, the

area commander from Bhagwanpur, Kharik Dusadh, was asked to brief the chief about his area. He was a dark, short, middle-aged man. In the dim light of the lantern, his white teeth glistened.

'There is a person called Chamtu Mahto in our area, who was earlier with us. He was an informant for us in our operation against the mukhia of Bishanpur village, but now he has become a police informant,' Kharik Dusadh said.

'So, what are you going to do about him?' the chief asked.

'He is our enemy number one. But he tends to stick to the area around the police station. He goes to the village at odd hours and then informs the police about us.'

'Have you planned to eliminate him?'

'Yes. We have been following his movements but he has become very careful. We almost nabbed him once in the haat but he took advantage of the crowd and we could not open fire as it would have caused a large number of casualties of innocent people. Since then, he has not left the vicinity around the police station in Bhagwanpur.'

'You should not delay once you have decided to eliminate him.'

Thus the meeting went on. Each area commander spoke in turn. They discussed issues of ideology, their struggle, and their impact on the political and cultural front. It was then time to chalk out a future plan of action. The chief announced the orders from the high command:

'There is a shortage of food in the interiors of the area. The poor are unable to get a meal even once a day. This is the time to gain their support. We will take possession of the grain godowns belonging to both the government and individual mill owners. We will involve the people in our operations, in fact, put them in the forefront and have our armed squad only provide support. We will distribute the grain amongst the people who come with us and ask them to carry away as much grain as possible. Our area commanders will chalk out a plan for their respective areas – I want you all to identify the godowns we can target, mobilize the people in your area and lead these groups. We have to convince the people that the grain actually belongs to them. It is just the exploitative machinery of the state that allows a few people to amass the grains and store them in godowns,' the chief paused and looked around, 'Any questions?'

Nobody raised any.

The chief spoke again, 'Today's last resolution is specifically for the area commander of the trans-Kareh area. We have information that the village head of Bhagatpur is the main rallying point against us. Their Mukhia is forming an armed group to fight us. He is collecting arms for this purpose and mobilizing support from his caste. The police is also reportedly supporting him. He was the main person behind the killing of innocent people in Dhobi Tola, but the police didn't arrest him, saying that there was no evidence. His atrocities on the poor people of Tesri are not hidden from us. The party command has decided to have Achal Singh eliminated. The area commander of trans-Kareh has to finish this job as soon as possible.'

The meeting lasted till two in the morning.

26.

Later that evening, everyone from Tesri had congregated at the graveyard. Israfil Mian's father, Shariff Mian, had suddenly died at two-thirty that afternoon when all the male members were out of the house. When Israfil Mian had left for his teashop at the haat in the morning his father had been hale and hearty. Shariff Mian was well over seventy, yet looking at him nobody would have guessed he would die just like that.

Shariff Mian had gone to offer prayers in the mosque that afternoon with no premonition of what lay ahead. He had come back from the mosque and asked his daughter-in-law to serve him lunch in his room. When his daughter-in-law went to his room with his lunch on a tray a short while later, she found him sleeping with his face to the wall. She set the tray down on the table near the bed and tried to wake him. That is when she realized he was not breathing. She felt for his pulse – nothing. His body was already cold. She ran outside, crying, 'He is dead! He is dead!'

Within minutes, the house was full of people and the women of the neighbourhood started wailing their lament. Somebody grabbed a bicycle and hurried to the haat to inform Israfil Mian. By the time he came home, everyone from the village had already collected.

It was almost evening when they lifted the dead body onto a bamboo cot for the final journey to the graveyard. As was the tradition in Tesri, everyone, irrespective of their caste or religion, was present. They carried a gaslight whose flame got extinguished by a sudden gust of wind.

When the people were praying for the departed soul after the burial, Jamuna Das was accosted by some strangers. One of them, a slightly built man in a checked lungi and blue shirt said: 'Pawan has sent us to talk to you. We are from Ibrahimpur.'

Jamuna Das dreaded talking to the Maoists. He knew there was going to be trouble. 'But where can we talk? Nobody is going to sit under the banyan tree today as we are in mourning,' he said.

The man moved away to confer with his friends. There were four of them in all. After a while he came back and said, 'Tell your people to come to the meeting place. We are very busy. We have to go to other villages as well.'

So despite a death in the village, everybody gathered under the banyan tree. Since the village was in mourning, Jamuna Das did not bring his radio. The man who had spoken to Jamuna Das earlier started his address as soon as they were all there:

'As you know, we are fighting against the atrocities perpetrated on us by the landlords of the area. Since they are out to kill us, we have taken up arms against them. They have the support of the government and the police. They try to kill us, to maim us, to exterminate us. But we have survived and, in fact, we are growing stronger – all because of the support of people like you. We take up the cause of the downtrodden; those who have nothing to lose but their suffering. I know that the landlords of Bhagatpur have always exploited the people of this village. But do not worry. We are with you. We will fight your battle. We will avenge your humiliation. And you must support us in the struggle.'

The man seemed to be something of a novice; he was not a confident speaker. He stopped now and then, muffing his lines, and peering at the people whose faces could not be seen in the dim light of the lantern. No one said anything and the speaker was unable to judge whether the people were responding to his call to arms. But he plodded through his speech, regardless:

'The government has stored away foodgrain for the poor but it has not been distributed to us, and we are dying of hunger. The fair-price shops are run by contractors who charge higher prices for the grain and often sell off the stock in the black-market. Therefore our party high command has decided that we will take possession of all foodgrain godowns. Those of you who are our supporters should accompany us and carry away as much grain as you can. We will be going with our armed squad who will ensure that nothing happens to anyone of you. All of you, men and women, are invited to join us. You have nothing to lose but your hunger.'

He stopped and looked around expectantly but his audience refused to respond. After a long awkward pause Bhagat Ram finally asked, 'What do you want us to do?'

The man who had been speaking looked at his three companions who were sitting next to him. Just then, Chowkidar Chedi Paswan arrived and walked towards the gathering. Seeing him, Jamuna Das lost his nerve. He got up and moved towards Chedi Paswan to take him aside and warn him about the presence of the Maoists. But before he could, the Maoist speaker, who seemed to know the chowkidar, said, 'Let him come here and listen to us, even if he is a chowkidar.'

Chedi Paswan sat down quietly.

The man continued: 'All that you people need to do is to join us in large numbers. Don't worry about the landlords or the police. We will take care of both of them.'

The four of them left soon after, without waiting to hear what the people had to say. They seemed confident that a large number of people would accompany them on their mission.

27.

By December each year the people of Tesri were near starvation. They earned grain instead of wages for working the fields of Bhagatpur's landowners and the crops they reaped from their own small patches of land at the end of the rainy season, saw them through only three or four months. By November their meagre supplies would begin to peter out. When winter crept in on them they would have next to nothing to eat. That was the time of the year when the able-bodied among them went to the cities to find work, any kind of work, so that they could send some money to their families back home.

In such a situation, the Maoists' call to join them in their plunder of foodgrain was given serious consideration; though none was about to openly admit it.

Soon many people from Tesri and Dhobi Tola quietly joined the Maoists and went with them in the hope of getting some food. The Maoists raided the grain godowns of the government – where grain was ostensibly stored to sell to the people at subsidized rates, or for their food-for-work programmes. They also raided rice mills owned by big businessmen. The Maoists convinced the people that the grain kept in storage was meant for them and was sold in the black-market by corrupt government officials.

People living in abject poverty are easy to convince.

Every time a raid was planned the villagers were informed and were told to gather at a designated spot. Many villagers from neighbouring villages joined in as well. Though all the villagers present knew each other, they pretended not to. They knew that what they were doing was highly risky and against the law and if the police caught them they could get arrested, sent to jail, or even killed. Their only interest in these missions was getting a few kilos of grain for themselves.

The villagers were escorted by an armed squad until, at the agreed-upon place of action, the Maoists opened fire. Then the villagers grabbed whatever they could and ran back to a predetermined spot. From here they dispersed after a head-count and a lecture from the Maoists.

The villagers were very circumspect about their nightly adventures and discussed their participation strictly only with those others whom they had seen at the looting. They did not breathe a word of it to anyone else. Still everyone in the village knew exactly who all had gone on each mission and what they had brought back.

Jamuna Das was the only person in Tesri who disagreed with the looting of the government's godowns. As always, he did not express his opinion about this but waited to see what the others' reaction was.

The village elders were surprised how quickly the whole village had come under the influence of the Maoists.

28.

Lately, the otherwise eventless life of Bhagatpur had been doubly beset with troubles. Though the threat from the Maoists had united the villagers for a while, the long standing trial of the criminal case between Achal Singh Mukhia and Pratap Singh had finally reached its concluding stage and was creating a divide between the two groups of the village again. Mukhia wanted to delay the ruling. But despite his attempts, the judge had fixed a date for the final judgement.

Most of Bhagatpur's villagers had forgotten the incident that had taken place so many years ago.

That bloody Saturday, more than twenty years ago, which had left one person dead and many injured, had faded from the memory of all, except the two families who fought the case tooth and nail in court.

After Pratap Singh had left the village, leaving behind only a few relatives and supporters, Achal

Singh Mukhia's influence over the village had strengthened. Over the years, Achal Singh Mukhia had been sending his loyalists to follow up the case with his lawyers whenever there was a hearing in the court. His tactics had always been to delay the trial. But after Lakhan Subedar had spoken to his ex-CO in the army, who was a cousin of the presiding judge, the judge had taken up the trial on a priority basis.

Two of Mukhia's trusted men – who were also co-accuseds in the case – were camping in the district headquarters. They had sent information that the verdict was likely to go against them. Hearing this, the mukhia was unnerved and decided to go to the district headquarters himself to somehow prevent an adverse verdict.

⌘

It was early December. The sky was a clear blue and Mukhia's east-facing veranda was full of the mild winter sun of early morning. Achal Singh sat in his reclining chair, wearing his trademark white kurta and pyjama. His white beard glistened in the sun. Despite his advancing years and the growing threat of the Maoists that had shaken his morale, his face retained the ruddy glow of youth. As usual, the veranda in Mukhia's house was full of people. His sympathizers were concerned about the outcome of the case that could technically send Mukhia to jail for an unspecified period.

The people were discussing the case and expressing their sympathy towards him, but Achal Singh hardly responded. He was known to become a man of few words during times of crises.

'The priest of the temple is ready for the yagna,' a villager came up to him and said.

Mukhia got up from his chair and walked proudly – head held erect – all the way to the village temple that was situated on an elevation on the outskirts of the village, in a clearing surrounded by banyan and peepal trees.

Beyond the temple, past large tracts of wheat fields, lay the hamlet of Dhobi Tola. Whenever there was a ceremony in the temple the women and children of Dhobi Tola would watch curiously from the outskirts of their village. On that day too, they stood at the edge of their Tola and watched as Achal Singh Mukhia went inside the temple and sat cross-legged in front of the statue of Lord Hanuman.

The pujari started chanting mantras. Mukhia's retinue remained outside on the veranda of the temple. Soon burning incense and the chant of Vedic hymns rose through the air.

His eyes closed in prayer, Mukhia thought back to the incident from long ago. He had forgotten the exact date but he remembered it had been a Saturday. All bad things in his life happened on Saturdays, he thought. He and Pratap Singh were in dispute over a piece of land that had ultimately not come under either's possession and now lay fallow.

That day, more than twenty years ago, he had gone to take possession of the land with his supporters, armed with clubs and spears. He had assessed the situation wrongly. He had assumed that nobody in the village would challenge him and he was confident that there would be no resistance from Pratap Singh. On reaching the disputed plot he had been surprised to see Pratap Singh coming from the opposite direction with his supporters – mostly men from other villages – who were armed too. Mukhia knew that if he retreated now he would lose face. And once the fight started nobody could control the consequences.

The results of that bloody Saturday proved to be far-reaching for Achal Singh Mukhia. Ramadhar Singh, Pratap Singh's cousin, died from head injuries sustained during the fight. The police were called. Mukhia was forced to go underground to evade arrest despite the fact that he was village headman. After several months of lying low he surrendered in court and went to jail. He was released on bail after three months. After that, the trial had taken such a very long time that even he had forgotten that he was an accused in a murder trial.

He had assumed the trial would go on forever. Now the likelihood of a verdict being reached, and that it could be a negative one at that, had completely thrown him.

The priest of the temple got up and applied a spot of vermilion to Mukhia's forehead. 'Lord Hanuman will make you victorious,' he said.

Mukhia stood up, went near the statue of Lord Hanuman, and prostrated himself. For the first time in his life, he felt helpless. He prayed, 'Save me from further humiliation.'

On the way home from the temple his followers and he walked past the abandoned property of Pratap Singh, and next to it, that of his cousins'. Someone in the crowd shouted, 'We will win!' Mukhia looked back sternly and said, 'No shouting please. This is not the time for slogans.'

⌘

Mukhia left on foot for Dumri at ten-thirty, from where he planned to take a bus. A large group of his supporters accompanied him all the way up to the haat. Mukhia stopped at the police picket that had been set up there after the massacre in Dhobi Tola.

The picket-in-charge came out of his makeshift office and greeted him: 'Ram-ram Mukhiaji! Where are you going?' He was an old policeman with a wrinkled face but still looked fit.

Mukhia sat on a wooden chair with a broken armrest and thought for a moment, all the while looking intently at the old cop. Lately, after the massacre in Dhobi Tola and with the growing influence of the Maoists in the area, he had stopped telling his programme to anyone except his wife, who suffered from dementia anyway and couldn't even remember that her husband was sitting next to her unless she saw him.

But that day everybody in the village knew the mukhia was going to the district headquarters in connection with his case. There was no point being secretive about his destination.

'I am going to Puraini,' he said.

'Take care. The whole area is crawling with Maoists,' the old policeman said.

About a dozen of Mukhia's acolytes still hung around. Some of them drifted off towards Israfil Mian's teashop. Being Saturday, the haat was not crowded.

'Have a cup of chai, Mukhiaji. You must always accept when you are offered a cup at the beginning of a journey. Otherwise, it is a bad omen,' the picket-in-charge said.

When the mukhia didn't reply he shouted across to Israfil Mian's boy who promptly brought across tea in glasses.

'How is the overall situation?' Mukhia asked taking a sip. At the back of his mind, he feared for his safety during the journey.

'On the face of it everything is peaceful but nobody can be sure with the Maoists. They attack their targets at the oddest places and at the most unexpected times.'

Mukhia gulped down his tea, which had already become cold, placed the glass on the ground and stood up. 'If I get killed, my next generation will be much stronger,' he said.

The picket in-charge looked at him admiringly and thought, 'Wah! Mukhia has nerves of steel.'

⌘

By the time Mukhia left for Dumri, the people accompanying him had dwindled to five. It was a walk of almost three miles on a deserted mud road that was even more quiet that day. Occasionally, after long stretches, a lone cyclist went past. The sky was deep blue and cloudless. Being winter the sun was not harsh. Mukhia enjoyed the cool breeze against his face.

Till a few months ago, he would not have feared travelling by that mud road. He would have walked back to his village without a thought, even in the middle of the night. Now, he had five persons escorting him, two of whom carried licensed weapons while the other three had unlicensed revolvers concealed under their shirts. But the mukhia was still insecure. How would he react if the Maoists attacked? Would he beg for his life? Or would he ask his men to fight back? He was praying for a safe passage just till Dumri. The bus journey from Dumri to the district headquarters did not frighten him. A large number of passengers on the bus and the presence of the police patrol on the state highway meant the Maoists would be less likely to attack him.

Hoping to chase away his negative thoughts, he turned his attention to the farmland on both sides of the road. The green fields glittered like emeralds; they looked beautiful.

After a while they approached the village of Jamua, which marked the halfway point between his village and Dumri. Mukhia felt relieved that he had covered half the distance safely. He decided to rest for a while near an old well by the village. One of his escorts pulled up some water. Mukhia washed his face and then cupped his palms to gulp mouthfuls of it. A bullock-cart laden with women and children trundled past. The canopy of the cart was torn and the women seated inside were visible. The children perched behind the bullock-cart were laughing. Mukhia relaxed and smiled at the kids.

'There is not even a teashop on this three-mile stretch,' one of the escorts complained.

In earlier days, Mukhia used to stop at Jamua on the way to Bhagatpur. He would chat with the village head and have a cup of tea with him, and only after resting for a while would he proceed. But now, even the situation in this village had changed.

'We should keep moving and reach Dumri as early as possible,' another escort said.

They got up and started walking again. There was nobody on the road for as far as they could see. The sun shone directly above now. Mukhia felt beads of sweat roll off his forehead. He looked at the sky. He had still to walk a mile and half. He did not feel like moving further, he wanted to sit down. He realized that he was no longer as young as he used to be and promised himself that, if everything went well, he would never again venture out of his village.

Half a mile from Jamua was the most isolated stretch on the route with a row of mango orchards on both sides of the road. The orchards were so dense that it looked dark even in the daytime. Mukhia thought that if he crossed this patch he would reach Dumri safely because beyond the orchards the road was fairly busy.

Suddenly a dozen men in police uniforms stepped out of the orchards. For a second, he thought they were really policemen. But the next moment they had encircled Mukhia and his escorts and were aiming their weapons at them. It was so sudden that none of his escorts could react.

They shouted, 'Drop your guns.'

One of his escorts tried to take out the pistol from under his shirt. The next moment he lay in a pool of blood.

'If anyone else tries any stunts, he is going to be dead.'

Mukhia legs were trembling so hard he thought he would fall. He realized that they were either going to kidnap him or kill him then and there. All his life he had not been a coward and had led his people with bravery, he thought. He would not die a coward.

He hid his fright and looked straight into the eyes of their leader. It was a young man. He recognized him with a start. Ramu Hajjam's son. Mukhia had heard that he had gone underground with the Maoists, but he had never imagined that they would meet like this.

Pawan turned to address the mukhia's men, 'We are only against the exploiters. Tell everyone in the village: if anyone acts like the mukhia, he will suffer the fate of Mukhia.'

Then he nodded to one of the Maoists who walked up to Mukhia and shot him at point-blank range.

⌘

Pawan and his gang of Maoists picked up the weapons that the escorts had dropped on the ground, tossed some pamphlets that said, 'This is our judgment against all exploiters', on the mukhia's corpse, and, as suddenly as they had come, disappeared back into the dark of the mango groves.

29.

For several moments after the assailants disappeared, Mukhia's men were too numb to react. Mukhia's head had been blown away; his blood and brains lay splattered about. They tried to feel his pulse. Then they realized that they were fooling themselves. All the four started shouting for help.

It was only after thirty minutes that a man who was on his way to Dumri, stopped. He was Rampukar Singh from Bhagatpur and he had started for Dumri half an hour after Mukhia. When he saw the bodyguards shouting for help he ran all the way to Jamua to get assistance.

An hour later a large group of people had gathered around. As there was no speculation about who had killed Mukhia, they were all tight-lipped. They didn't even discuss how the assailants came upon them, opened fire and ran back into the orchards. They saw the leaflets left by the Maoists and made no attempt to touch the dead body.

The chowkidar of Jamua, with his red turban and long bamboo stick, showed up eventually and took charge of the scene of the crime. He shouted at the over-inquisitive and moved them away from the spot.

⌘

The police arrived at around three. They left their vehicles at Dumri Chowk and walked down the mud road to the crime spot fearing that the Maoists might have laid explosives on the road.

The police officer first inspected the body of the mukhia and then that of his bodyguard. He examined the wound on Mukhia's skull carefully. The exit wound was very big, clearly showing that the brain had been ripped apart. The impact of the bullet was so immense that it had shattered the skull scattering shards of bone all over the ground. The police officer then focused on the area around the dead body and found two empty cartridges and picked up the leaflets left by the Maoists.

'Get the papers and do the formalities,' he said to a junior officer who was assisting him.

The junior officer called the chowkidar and asked him to turn over the mukhia's body to see whether it bore any more injuries. After inspecting both the dead bodies, he filled out the forms he was carrying. Meanwhile, the police officer went towards the people assembled under the tree a few metres away.

'Was anybody present at the time of incident?' he asked.

The four bodyguards of the deceased came forward. They were still in shock. The police officer took them aside and talked to each of them separately. The officer got the whole story from them. He was astonished to find out that a young boy called Pawan from Tesri was the leader of the Maoist assailants.

While he was talking to the guards, a large group of people arrived from Bhagatpur and merged with the crowd that waited under the tree. They were very agitated. Some of them carried clubs and started shouting slogans against the police.

'If any of you want to fight the Maoists, you are welcome. But don't shout slogans here, at this time,' the police officer yelled back at them. Then he said, 'Is there any relative of the deceased Mukhia present among you?'

A man in his late forties came forward. He was Ashok Singh, Mukhia's nephew, who looked after Mukhia's property. He was an unimpressive fellow who spoke with a distinct stammer – most unlike the mukhia. Though he seemed harmless and innocent, the villagers knew him to be cunning and shrewd. He ran to the officer and started howling: 'My father is dead. My father is dead.'

The police officer took him aside to talk to him in confidence. 'We have to register a case to investigate further and you have to decide who will give us the statement for this.'

The four bodyguards and Ashok Singh looked at each other. Then Ashok Singh said, 'We have to discuss this amongst ourselves before we reach a decision.' They went back to the crowd, made a small huddle and quibbled over the issue.

The police officer busied himself supervising the work of his junior officer. After a while the police officer tried to locate the mukhia's nephew and the bodyguards. They were taking a long time.

'Please send the bodyguards and Ashok Singh over at once,' he shouted to the crowd.

They came up to him. The police officer took one look at them and knew instinctively that they were going to concoct a cock-and-bull story.

'What have you decided?' he asked them. No one replied. Clearly none wanted to take the lead. The officer wanted to slap Ashok Singh. 'Have you all been struck dumb?'

'The Maoists were probably not the assailants because one of the guards saw Pratap Singh hidden in the orchard when the assailants came,' Ashok Singh said, looking pointedly at one of the escorts, who began to tremble.

The officer was outraged. 'Have some shame! Don't involve an innocent in this murder case.' Their version of the story left him seething. He had talked to all the three guards separately and not once had anyone mentioned Pratap Singh. One of the guards had even taken Pawan's name; he had immediately recognized him as he had seen him at Ramu Hajjam's shop. And the officer knew from experience that the Maoists never made any attempt to conceal their identity when shooting down their targets.

He looked with stern eyes at the guard who was still shivering. 'What did you see? Tell me again,' the officer thundered.

'Uh…I saw Pratap Singh… come up to the side of the road while the assailants – around seven in number – encircled us, killed Mukhia and our friend and ran away... Pratap Singh also went with them back inside the orchard,' the guard said haltingly.

The police officer felt a deep revulsion for the men. Before he had left for Dumri, where his jeep was parked, he had seen Pratap Singh sitting in his hotel, talking to customers. In all his years in the police force, he had never once seen a suspect return to his house after committing a murder and get busy with the daily chores. He was aware of the long-standing feud between Mukhia and Pratap Singh.

'You people should be ashamed of yourselves! If you act like this the Maoists will soon take over the whole area,' the police officer said, walking away in disgust.

30.

Earlier only a single sentry stood on duty at the entry point of the police camp in the haat, but after news spread that the Maoists were behind the attack on the mukhia, security was fortified. All the constables who were relaxing inside the tent, pulled on their uniforms, grabbed their rifles, and took position around the camp. The officer of the group was the first one to come out, buttoning his holster to his belt, and sat himself down on the lone chair in the courtyard.

By two in the afternoon, news of Mukhia's murder had reached the haat on its way to Bhagatpur. Nobody believed it at first but then they witnessed the frantic activity in the makeshift police camp and realized, with growing fear, that the news was true.

⌘

'Achal Singh Mukhia is dead! He was killed near Jamua,' Anwar Mian came running from his bicycle repair shop to tell Ramu Hajjam.

Ramu Hajjam was sitting idly, lost in thought, on the ground near the small temple that he had made next to his shop. He hadn't shaved since Pawan had left home. His long beard shone in the sun.

'Who killed him?' he asked.

'I don't know. I am going to Israfil Mian's teashop to find out. Everybody is collecting there.'

'I am sitting here. You go and find out.'

Then a horrible thought struck Ramu Hajjam: What if his son were involved in the killing of Mukhia? He looked at the small figurine of Lord Hanuman that he had enshrined in the small brick structure he called his temple. He felt restless. 'Come back quickly. There is going to be trouble. We should head home as soon as possible,' he said to Anwar Mian.

Anwar Mian walked across to the teashop. Everyone there was discussing the incident and its consequences. Speculations about who was *really* responsible for killing Mukhia were rife even though everyone knew that an armed squad of the Maoist group had killed him. After a few minutes there, Anwar Mian remembered that Ramu Hajjam was waiting for him under the neem. Since there was nothing more to be had by way of specific information at the teashop, he went back to his stall.

'Better to wind up for the day. There will not be any more customers now,' he said to Ramu.

Ramu Hajjam and Akbar Mian packed away their tools and then went back to the teashop where the people were still engrossed in animated discussion. But seeing Ramu Hajjam, a silence fell upon them.

Ramu Hajjam felt odd. Anwar Mian was embarrassed by the sudden silence that welcomed his friend. 'Let's go,' he said, catching hold of Ramu Hajjam's hand and led him away.

They walked in silence all the way to their village. Ramu Hajjam was visibly worried. Anwar Mian felt worried for him. On reaching the village they found some policemen relaxing on the platform under the banyan. Chowkidar Chedi Paswan was with them. Ramu Hajjam could not hide his anxiety when Chedi said, 'I will come and talk to you soon.' He requested Anwar Mian to come along with him to his house.

Ramu Hajjam and Anwar Mian were sitting on a cot in the courtyard, nervously sipping tea, when Chedi Paswan arrived at Ramu Hajjam's house, a while later. He too looked tired and distressed. Chedi Paswan rested his staff by the charpoy and lowered himself onto it. 'Life as a chowkidar has become miserable,' he said.

'What has happened? Why are you looking so harassed?' Anwar Mian asked.

'Now the police will stay in the village for God knows how many days. The police coming to the village just compounds problems for a poor chowkidar like me. We don't require any security from anyone but they think that Achal Singh Mukhia's men will retaliate by attacking us.' Chedi Paswan was breathing heavily, a sure sign of an impending asthma attack. He wheezed hard.

Ramu Hajjam called out to his wife and asked her to get a cup of tea for Chedi Paswan.

'Despite the presence of the police, most of the people have left Tesri fearing a backlash from the landlords of Bhagatpur,' Chowkidar said as he took a sip of the tea that Phulmani brought him.

'I think I too better go home and see whether all is well there,' Akbar Mian said, standing up abruptly,

'Don't worry. Nobody from Kunjra Toli has left the village. Either they are expecting no backlash, or they have decided not to leave their houses in fear,' Chowkidar told him.

Ramu Hajjam sipped his tea in silence. He knew there would be more trouble after the mukhia's death because he was the one person who had had a hold on the people of Bhagatpur. Everyone had approached him for resolving disputes; he had been the only one capable of controlling the unruly people of his village. Now everyone would want to be the leader.

'Mukhia's dead body will be brought to the village tomorrow. We will have to assess the situation then. The people of Bhagatpur are also afraid right now. If the Maoists can kill the mukhia, they can kill anyone,' Chowkidar explained, setting his empty cup on the floor.

The involvement of the Maoists in Mukhia's murder scared Ramu Hajjam. He knew that Pawan was one of them, but he had no idea how high his position in the organization was. He would never have imagined that his son had become an area commander in such a short time. He assumed he was probably a small-time functionary, a mere foot soldier participating in processions and mobilizing people in support of the organization.

Then Chedi said, 'The police were asking about your son. They were asking whether he visits his house. I said nobody has seen him after he left the village.'

The information didn't affect Ramu Hajjam; it was not the first time that the police had come asking about his son. They had come before, in the night, searching every nook and corner of his house, threatening him and asking him irrelevant questions, but he had never considered his son a criminal and therefore had never felt guilty.

'What were they saying about my son?' Ramu Hajjam asked.

'They are saying that he was the leader of the team that killed Achal Singh Mukhia.'

Ramu felt a piercing pain in his heart. He collapsed onto the charpoy, and barely noticed when Chedi and Akbar Mian left the house. His mind was a whirl. He felt it float away into a distant dream...

In his dream, he saw a great saint with a halo around his head, his shining face emanating absolute peace. The saint was sitting on a high pedestal adorned with beautiful carvings and a group of people were sitting on the ground, facing him. Once again Ramu Hajjam found himself present in the audience.

And the saint was telling the story of a lizard who

had been cheated on by his friend, the chameleon. There was a young lizard, son of the king of lizards, whose family resided on the riverbank in the jungle. His closest friend was a chameleon. The lizard's father had advised the young lizard to stay away from her since chameleons were lowly creatures and untrustworthy. However, the young lizard didn't heed the advice of his father and continued his friendship. The lizard's father, finding no change in the behaviour of his son and foreseeing danger, constructed a secret tunnel in the young lizard's burrow so that he could escape quickly if needed.

As they grew older, the chameleon remained small whereas the lizard grew big. Now the embraces of the lizard were painful to the chameleon. She thought, if they continued like this, she would die one day. So, the chameleon decided to get not only the lizard killed but also to destroy the whole tribe of lizards.

It so happened that one day a lizard trapper came to the jungle with his dog. The chameleon immediately conspired with the trapper and showed him the burrows of the lizards, and told him to smoke them at one end and stand ready with sticks and the dog at the other. Thus the trapper caught a large number of lizards. However, the young lizard escaped to safety through the secret tunnel that his father had made. He realized that his father had been correct. An animal like a chameleon, known for its wickedness and treachery, can never be a reliable and trusted friend.

At that moment Ramu Hajjam wanted to get up and ask the saint: 'And what will happen to my son?

He trusted people who believe in violence. They have made him kill somebody. I want to know whether they will protect him or not. He is my child, my only son. I want him back. Tell me, what will happen to him?'

But then he saw in his dream that neither the saint nor the people were there. He tried to run but total darkness engulfed him. He woke drenched in sweat, only to find Phulmani sitting at the door that lead to the veranda, deep in thought.

A lantern hung from the door frame, right over her head.

Even though his wife of many years sat near him Ramu Hajjam felt intensely alone.

31.

Murli Compounder had been attending to a patient when his assistant Upendra barged in screaming: 'Mukhia is dead! He was killed on his way to Puraini!'

The patient with him was a Maoist leader who had introduced himself as Amar from Saadipur village. Murli knew that the patient had disclosed neither his actual name nor his real address. The man had a deep gash on his ankle and claimed he'd fallen on the sharp edge of a spade. Murli had not believed that story either.

The wound was infected right up to the bone and had turned gangrenous. The patient had been staying in his clinic for over a week, along with an attendant. This had led Murli to believe that the patient was not an ordinary Maoist but a leader of the organization. His attendant took care of all his needs, cooking his meals and serving them to him.

Murli was squatting on the ground and cleaning Amar's wound. The smell of the putrefying wound mingled with that of the disinfectant. He had been so lost in his work that he hadn't heard what Upendra said. He looked up at him inquiringly.

'Mukhia is dead,' Upendra said again.

Murli had got up from the ground in disbelief. He sensed there would be more danger. 'Does anybody know who killed him?' he had asked.

'The Maoists. They came out of a mango orchard and shot him at point-blank range. One of Mukhia's bodyguards was also killed,' Upendra reported.

Murli had at down to resume dressing the wound and willed himself to focus. Since he had already opened the wound he couldn't leave it. He was surprised to see how quickly the wound was healing. He washed the cut with antiseptic, placed some cotton gauze smeared with antibiotic cream over it, and tied a fresh bandage. Then he stood up, washed his hands and came back to his chair.

Murli looked at the prescription he had written. 'You need to continue oral antibiotics for another six days. We will continue to dress the wound twice a week. Hopefully you will be able to walk properly in the next couple of days.'

Amar had remained seated on the stool, expressionless. After a while he said, 'How much do I owe you?'

'I will tell you when you leave this place.'

'Well now, because of the mukhia's murder, I might have to leave earlier.'

'That is your choice. But the police do not harass patients unless there is specific information about them.'

'In that case, I would rather stay here.'

'Yes, it is best if you go when you are able to walk,' Murli said.

After Amar left his room, Murli had pondered the fall-out of the murder. Since the Maoists were involved, the blame would come to rest, directly or indirectly, on the three boys of Tesri who had gone underground. He was worried about Pawan who had been training so well under him. He guessed that right now all the villagers would be gathered under the banyan discussing the killing. He too had locked his clinic and gone off towards the banyan tree.

A mild December afternoon sun filtered through the leaves of the tree. Under them, the village was in full attendance. Everyone present looked deeply worried. Even the young boys of the village sat around grimly, for once listening quietly to every word being spoken. Murli Compounder had sat himself in a corner.

Jagat Ram was saying, 'When the body of Mukhia is brought back to the village his supporters will go berserk and attack us.'

'People are saying that Pawan was the main assailant. It was he who opened fire on him. The other people with him recognized him,' Amrit Lal said.

'Pawan has become a big leader in their organization. He must be closely involved in the killing of Mukhia,' Jagat Ram opined.

'But what are we going to do? This attack puts us all at risk. The killings in Dhobi Tola happened because the Maoists had attacked Bhagatpur on the eve of elections, and Mukhia's goons retaliated,' Mangat Ram said. He was an old man and well respected in the village because though he spoke rarely, he spoke wisely.

Lakhan Subedar thought of his humiliation by Achal Singh Mukhia. He was happy he had spoken to his ex-CO. He was happy that he had been killed like this. He said, 'Nothing will happen this time. Mukhia deserved this kind of death. With him gone, there is no one in Bhagatpur who has the guts to attack us. We should rejoice at his demise.'

Sitting in the centre of the gathering, with no radio beside him, Jamuna Das listened quietly, absorbing everybody's comments

Just then the villagers saw a posse of policemen walking towards them. There were ten of them in all, a few with their rifles on their shoulders, the rest holding them like staffs. They looked tired and dejected. They walked up to the tree and the people shifted to make space for them. Jamuna Das asked his boy to bring them some water. The in-charge of the police party – the proud owner of a flamboyant, well-oiled and curled moustache – wiped the dust from his face with a cotton gamcha tucked in his uniform belt. Then he asked the gathering, 'Why are you people all sitting here? Are you planning something?'

Jamuna Das realized that he should come forward and speak for them all. 'The villagers are scared that they might be attacked by the supporters of Achal Singh Mukhia. They are planning to flee the village tonight,' he said.

The police officer had been camping at the haat for the last three months and was well aware of the dynamics of the region. He knew that if the police hadn't been camping there, the villagers of Tesri would have fled to a secure place long ago.

'Don't worry. We are going to stay here for some time. Nobody will dare attack the people of Tesri with us around,' he said, but his words carried little conviction.

A young man said, 'They killed women and children in Dhobi Tola right under your nose. What is the guarantee we will be secure?'

The police officer knew he wouldn't be able to convince the villagers to stay in the village but he had orders from his officer. He had been commanded to pitch base there with a posse of armed constables. He needed to find a place to stay for a couple of weeks or, at least, till the tension between the two villages subsided. 'Where in this mohalla can we people stay for couple of days?' he asked Jamuna Das.

Jamuna Das looked pointedly at Murli Compounder who just as deliberately ignored his gaze. He knew that Jamuna Das wanted him to let the police stay in the shed that served as a waiting room for his patients.

'Unfortunately, there is not a single proper house in the village where ten–twelve constables can be put up together,' Jamuna Das said at last, realizing that Murli was not going to offer his premises.

Suddenly Chedi Paswan, who had been standing behind the policemen, piped in, 'We can fix up the hut next to your shop. I will put a thick layer of hay on the ground and a sheet on top of that. All the constables can adjust in that room.' He looked at Jamuna Das seeking his approval.

⌘

Soon after, all the villagers dispersed except for the policemen, Chowkidar Chedi Paswan and Jamuna Das. The constables were looking anxious – worried about how to settle down for the night and yet remain alert in this area infested by Maoists. Chedi Paswan was despatched to fetch a bucket of water. The police officer pumped Jamuna Das for more information about the village.

'Who is this Pawan? I am told he is an Area Commander in the underground organization.'

'He is the son of Ramu Hajjam, a barber from this village who almost lost his mind after he was beaten up in the haat,' Jamuna Das replied.

'Does Pawan come to visit his family?'

'Nobody knows whether he comes or not. Nobody has seen him after he went underground.'

'Are there others from this village who have gone underground?'

'Two more boys became Maoists after Pawan. Nobody from the village has seen them after they went underground, either.'

Chedi Paswan returned with a bucket of water, carrying it with some difficulty. He thought, why on earth did Achal Singh Mukhia have to die at the hands of the Maoists, and why did the policemen have to choose to come to this village where there was no need of providing security? Now it would fall upon him to arrange everything for the police party – from a place to sleep, to utensils to cook their meal. Ultimately, he would have to beg and borrow from the villagers, all of whom were sure to run away from the village at night, fearing retribution from the landlords of Bhagatpur.

Evening had set in. The animals coming back from the grazing ground raised clouds of dust on the dirt road. Chedi was finding it difficult to breathe. Whenever things got tense, he felt an attack of asthma come on. He looked at the houses in his village. They were remarkably quiet. No smoke billowed from any of them, as no fires had been lit in the hearths.

The people of Tesri were lying low.

32.

The only person from Tesri to offer his condolences when Achal Singh Mukhia's body arrived from the district headquarters was Murli Compounder. Nobody in Tesri suspected where he was going because he had left the village on his bicycle, as he did routinely every day.

In Bhagatpur a massive crowd had gathered in front of the late Mukhia's veranda. His dead body, wrapped in a white sheet, was laid out on a bamboo cot. Incense sticks burned in all four corners of the cot. People queued up to file past the shrouded body with folded hands and then went to sit in the veranda or under the trees.

Murli Compounder parked his bicycle under one of the trees, pulled out his face towel from his plastic bag and wiped the dirt off his face. It was getting slightly windy and cold. He followed the people who were going towards the dead body and joined the queue, moving with the line. As he stood in front of the body he remembered that the mukhia, for all his faults, had always been a very co-operative patient and, contrary to his reputation, had always been kind to Murli.

He felt that whatever was happening in the village was not right and that the chain of events would cause the death of more innocent people.

Murli paid his respects to the dead man and then joined a small group of people sitting under the tree, waiting for the procession to the cremation grounds to start. Murli knew all of those present. They were small-time farmers from Bhagatpur. He sat on the ground and started to chat with them. The atmosphere was very sombre. People spoke in low voices; the mood was one of grief.

'How is the situation in other villages? You visit the neighbouring villages to see patients so you must know,' one of them asked Murli.

Murli knew the man well. His name was Devendra. He had visited his house only last month because his son had been suffering from typhoid. He even remembered the name of the boy, Vikas, who had a very high fever for more than a week. Ultimately, Murli had to ask him to buy some antibiotic capsules from the district headquarters. He knew that despite being a farmer who owned a couple of acres of land, Devendra had been hard-pressed to pay for the medicines.

'The situation in other villages is pretty bad. Even small-time farmers have been affected badly. They can't even cultivate their fields because of the insecurity,' Murli said.

'What will the poor do? We are also poor. Achal Singh Mukhia was a big landlord but what about us? We are almost like labourers. The only difference is that we work in our own fields. But how does that make us any more privileged? Despite our hard work, we just about manage to make ends meet. Why should *we* be the target of these Maoists just because we live in this village and happen to be the same caste as Mukhia?' Devendra Singh asked.

'Yes, we are all being forced into positions to which we aren't willing parties. We are not landlords; *our* forefathers never exploited anyone. We are suffering for no reason,' another man sitting next to Devendra said.

Murli was quiet. He agreed with them. He realized that because the Maoists came to him for medical treatment he was granted amnesty from them. Otherwise, since he too owned a couple of fields and a large herd of cattle his lot would have been no different from Devendra's.

He was aware that there was something deeply flawed about the whole conflict. He was not sure whether it was a lack of direction or a lack of understanding.

33.

For a long time after the mukhia's murder, an uneasy quietude hung over the two villages. People living in Bhagatpur and Tesri minded their own business and worked in their respective fields. Some of the small landholders were forced to abandon their land. The hostility between the two villages was instilled so deep that people were who were once friends and co-workers were now suspicious of each other.

Each day at five in the evening, when the westerly wind blew dust on the grounds of the haat the hawkers shut down their stalls, after having waited all day for customers who no longer came. Then the whole bazaar would be deserted except for Israfil Mian's teashop which really only remained open for the policemen who camped on the haat grounds in increasing numbers.

Beside them the Kareh flowed on without a thought, unmindful of the fact that the pyres of all those killed and yet to be killed in the spiralling conflict, were illuminating its banks.

⌘

One night, several months later, Murli Compounder heard the persistent barking of stray dogs in the street. The Maoists were back, he thought, with more patients. He was sleeping inside a mosquito net on the veranda as it was hot and humid indoors. Summer had ended and a few early showers of the rainy season had made the weather so unbearable that it was difficult to sleep.

The barking dogs reminded him of the very first time the Maoists had come to his clinic in the dead of night. That night the strays had chased the Maoists, barking all the while. Even when the exhausted dogs had retired to a corner, they hadn't stopped barking.

Such minor impediments had never deterred the Maoists. So that night too, when they knocked on his door a few times, Murli knew he had no option but to answer it. He picked up the torch that he always kept under his pillow and quietly opened the door. Three men stood outside. One of them had a woollen chador wrapped around his shoulders even in the sweltering heat.

'We have come to leave our friend with you,' one of them said.

Murli Compounder stood aside, holding the door open. There must be armed men behind them, he thought. 'Please have mercy on me. The patient can come in the daytime. The police is everywhere. They treat me as a harbourer of the Maoists and I don't have any support from you. They can send me to jail anytime.' He always pretended to the Maoists that the police were a great threat to him.

'Nothing will happen to you. The police move in the daytime, we move at night.'

The frail man had a coughing fit that went on and on. He went to spit into the bushes and when he came back he was completely out of breath. Murli Compounder immediately guessed he was suffering from tuberculosis.

'His name is Chander Passi. Before joining the Maoists he used to collect toddy from palm trees – which he sold, and consumed. Too much toddy has spoiled his liver and lungs. Now he is unable to live without medication. He will stay here and you will provide food and medicine to him.'

Murli Compounder listened to them but did not respond. It was an order, and he had to oblige. He could not argue with them. The patient could stay in the shed adjacent to his clinic, which he had got especially built for out-of-station patients who had to stay overnight. At that moment, all he wanted was for them to leave.

'All right,' he said.

They took the patient to an empty corner of the veranda where several charpoys were laid out in a row. Chander Passi sat on the charpoy, coughing all the while. One of the men accompanying him took some money out of his pocket and handed it to Murli.

'This is for his medicine and food. He will not leave here unless one of us comes to take him.'

Then, they left – and the dogs barked their protest once again.

Murli Compounder went inside his clinic and returned with his stethoscope. The patient was already lying on a cot. An unbearably foul smell of fermented toddy, sputum and clothes that had not been washed for months, emanated from him. Murli took out a bottle of Dettol from the almirah, smeared a cotton swab with it and stuck it behind his own ear to block the smell.

'Tomorrow you will have a bath even if you have a fever of a hundred and three,' he said.

Chander Passi was quite sick. When Murli Compounder placed the stethoscope on his chest, it sounded as if his chest was hollow inside. In the torchlight, his skin glowed translucently bloodless. Murli wondered how he had walked the long distance to his clinic. Without even an X-ray Murli was certain that Passi had tuberculosis. He wrote out a prescription, then took out four strips of medicine from his plastic bag and handed them to Passi.

'Take one tablet from each strip right now,' he said.

By the time he had finished with the patient the sky had turned grey in the east. It was July and the monsoons had just begun. Soon the sun would rise. He wanted to have a bath and, perhaps, a short nap to compensate for the sleepless night. He went to the hand pump in the courtyard of the house. He found his wife awake. 'The Maoists came again with more patients?' she enquired.

He never shared information about his patients with his wife and was surprised that she knew. Women have strange ways of finding out things, he thought. 'Yes. And be careful, he will be here a long while.' He could not lie.

'The police will not leave you if they find out.'

He filled a plastic bucket with water and carried it towards the small cement platform he had built around the hand-pump for washing and bathing. The mugful of cold water relaxed him. The fatigue of the night was washed away as was the awful smell. As he bathed he thought, 'Whose side am I on? The Maoists' or the landlords'?'

Contrary to his earlier belief, he realized he was certainly not with the Maoists. He had earned quite well during the last three years through his successful medical practice and wanted peace in the area so that he could establish a hospital like Sundaram's Arogyadham. But if the Maoists got whiff of his wealth they would take all his money. The philosophy of the Maoists was against his interests. At the same time, he could not live here without staying in the Maoists' good books.

He had to tread very, very carefully.

34.

By the next afternoon, Chander Passi had made himself comfortable in a corner of the long veranda. He had even hammered a few nails into the side of the wall to hang his clothes and other stuff. Outside the veranda was a makeshift hearth with some utensils for in-patients to use. Chander Passi had cooked himself some rotis, taken a bath and washed his clothes – he was already looking better. Now he took out a few pamphlets of Maoist literature which his party comrades had taught him to read.

Over the days he settled into a routine. When he tired of resting or reading, he would sit facing the wall and talk to himself. Murli Compounder realized that Passi was a social man and needed company. So whenever Murli Compounder was free, he would chat with him. After fifteen days, the men who had brought Chander Passi came back at night to meet Murli Compounder. When Murli opened the door he found them sitting on the charpoy next to Chander Passi. It was a full-moon night and Murli was worried that their presence in his clinic would be noticed by someone, but they looked very relaxed.

'Your medicines have really helped our comrade. He looks much healthier now,' one of them said.

Their demeanour made it clear to Murli that Chander Passi was an important person in their establishment. They sat for a long while, talking to each other and updating Chander Passi about the happenings in their organization. Then one of them pulled out a wad of notes from his bag and handed it to Murli. 'This is for your expenditure on the treatment. Comrade Passi should get the best medicine and food.'

Murli Compounder took the money and went back inside the house because he realized that they were talking about their revolutionary activities. He could not sleep despite his best efforts. Finally, hearing the strays barking in the street and knowing they had left, he went to his room. Chander Passi was sitting on his cot looking perturbed. The moonlight falling on his face made him look tired and wrinkled.

'Your comrades have given me three thousand rupees for your medication and other expenses. You can keep the money if you want,' Murli said.

'No, you keep the money. I might just have to leave this place without telling anyone. You can adjust the amount later if I have to go suddenly,' Chander Passi said. He seemed distraught. Something serious must have happened. Chander Passi had never before spoken about leaving the clinic.

'What's wrong?' he thought he may as well be blunt.

'Two of our senior comrades have been killed by the police. Nobody knew of their whereabouts. We are surprised how the police found out about them. There are some informants in our ranks, or some villagers whom we trust are passing on information to the police.'

'I hope nobody knows that you are here. Otherwise I too will be ruined,' Murli said.

When Chander looked at him his eyes seemed heavy, burdened with a sense of responsibility for Murli, but his words were charged: 'Our struggle cannot stop with the death of one or two leaders. We will continue to organize the forceful possession of rice mills and foodgrain godowns, and we will distribute the grain among the poor. In fact, the people of the villages will do this themselves, with our armed guards covering them. This will raise the morale of our men and the people too will start joining our struggle. Together we will be ready to take on the police.'

In his emotional state, Chander Passi was divulging secret information about his organization. Murli Compounder thought it might be dangerous to even know about it, but Chander Passi continued, 'We are going to attack a rice mill near Deori on the national highway at midnight on Sunday.'

Murli kept quiet. He didn't know what to say. For the first time he was privy to a secret of the Maoists. He remembered the police chief who had told him to pass on any information he got. And now he was in possession of some very important information.

Five days later, at midnight on Sunday, the Maoists were conspiring to attack a rice mill – and he knew which one. If he shared this information with the police chief, they could lay a trap. He wondered how to contact the chief. If he went to town suddenly and then the police ambushed the Maoists, Chander Passi would certainly get suspicious. He would be killed as mercilessly as Achal Singh Mukhia had been.

⌘

Murli could not sleep that night. He kept thinking about how to send the information to the police chief. He could not make up his mind. He fell asleep only in the early hours of the morning but had to get up soon because the harsh sun was beating down on his charpoy. It was very hot and humid. There was not the slightest trace of a breeze.

'You have been sleeping so late. Everybody is waiting for you,' his wife said, when he got out of bed.

'Is Upendra here?' he asked his wife. Like Pawan once had, Upendra helped out in the clinic, working as his assistant.

'Everyone is here. It is almost nine.'

Murli dressed hurriedly all the while thinking about what he would do.

He had no patients waiting for him when he went to the clinic, which was a relief. Then he noticed that Chander Passi was missing from his cot. Murli remembered how agitated Chander Passi had been the previous night, wanting to rejoin his comrades at the battlefront. He looked around and saw that his cloth bag was missing too. That confirmed his suspicion. Murli shouted to Upendra:'Chander Passi has gone somewhere. Look for him and bring him back if you find him.'

He himself went towards the banyan tree but he was pretty sure that Chander Passi had gone back to his hideout. Passi had left no address. He didn't even know whether Chander was his real name. If Chander had left in the wee hours of morning, he would have gone very far by now. He decided that there was no point in chasing him. Murli went back to his clinic and felt that, with Passi gone, he would have to seriously think about contacting the police chief.

Sunday midnight was only three days away.

⌘

When Chander Passi didn't return the next morning, Murli Compounder was certain that he would not come back. He wondered if he would ever see him again. Probably not. Chander Passi, with his swollen liver and hollow chest would die soon, on or off the battlefront, without medicine, rest and proper food. He wished he could come back for treatment; Murli had liked him for his honesty and sensitivity.

Till yesterday, he had thought he would send Upendra with a handwritten note in an envelope to Sundaram, who would then pass the message on to the police chief. But now, with Chander Passi gone, he thought it best to meet the chief personally and tell him about the Maoists' plan.

As he cycled down to the haat, Murli was very conscious of the danger of the job he was doing that day – one that might even go against the interests of the people of Tesri. He wanted to avoid meeting anyone on the way and was ready to lie if questioned about his visit to the district headquarters.

He parked his bicycle in the thatched-roof hut adjacent to Pratap Singh's teashop and went towards the cot where Pratap Singh sat. He knew that Pratap Singh had survived at that isolated bus-stop only because he had the support of the Maoists. Each night, when the highway was deserted and even the police avoided coming out of the police station, Pratap Singh's hotel would turn into a Maoist den.

'Where are you going Doctor sahib?' Pratap Singh asked.

'I am going to the town to buy medicine.'

'And what else is happening in the village?' Pratap Singh was always keen to know what was happening in Bhagatpur.

'The people in Bhagatpur are scared. They are even afraid of going to their fields. The murder of Achal Singh Mukhia has demoralized them.' Murli knew that this is what Pratap Singh wanted to hear.

'All this happened because of the exploitative policies of Achal Singh Mukhia. After all, how many years would the people suffer?'

Murli Compounder didn't want to give an opinion on things that would land him in trouble with one group or the other, so he tried to change the topic. 'How is your teashop running? Do the Maoists harass you too?' he asked.

'They don't harass those who are not exploiters. They do come here, have tea and go away.'

At that moment, the bus arrived at the bus-stop. Murli Compounder got up, picked up his plastic bag and said, 'I will try to come back today. If I get late I will stay overnight with you.'

He reached the police chief's residence at two pm. He showed the visiting card the chief had given him at the gate and was immediately taken to the chief's personal assistant who recognized him instantly. Luckily for him the place had no other visitors. The personal assistant asked him to sit and informed the police chief of his arrival. Soon he was called inside.

'What is the news from your area?' the police chief asked.

'I have got some specific information about the Maoists,' Murli said.

The police chief looked grim and took out his diary. When Murli told him about the Maoists' plan, he wrote everything down, then cross-checked every detail. Finally, he asked, 'How authentic is this information?'

'The person who told me is himself a leader in the organization,' Murli said.

The police chief looked at him assessingly for a while and then said, 'You rest assured. Your name will not figure anywhere.'

Murli came out of the police chief's chamber and left quickly for the bus-stand to catch the earliest bus to Dumri. Once more, he was lucky and found nobody from his village or even from Bhagatpur on the bus. When he got off, and went to fetch his bicycle from Pratap Singh's teashop, he saw him standing there. Pratap looked a bit surprised. 'How have you come back so soon?'

'I got the medicine at the first shop itself and decided to rush back home as there was nothing much to do,' he said and went towards the hut where he had parked his bicycle.

He was back in his village by evening.

When he passed the banyan tree where Jamuna Das and all the other villagers sat, he got off his bicycle, wished them and exchanged pleasantries. He behaved normal but felt guilty thinking what the consequences of informing the police chief might be.

35.

Nobody knew exactly how news that the Maoists had called the villagers to participate in the loot of a rice mill on Sunday night spread in Tesri. The information was circulated by word of mouth from one to another and, then, to everybody but nobody knew where it originated. Ever since Tesri had come under the influence of the Maoists, the villagers had been to so many lootings that they had lost count. The Maoists called such operations 'the distribution of the wealth of the rich amongst the poor'. After the exercise was over, the villagers would return home with a few kilograms of grain, feel scared for a day or two, and then forget their little adventure. The police had never come and, by and by, they had stopped fearing them. They began to believe that what the Maoists were doing was free of danger

The call to participate in the looting of a rice mill was an attractive one. Rumour was that the rice mill was the largest in the district and stored innumerable rice bags. The villagers were happy to participate. They knew that the area commander of the Maoists would deploy one of his men to escort them to the venue, so they waited eagerly for him.

At seven that evening, three men arrived in the village. They went straight to the banyan tree in the main chowk, as if they already knew the villagers were gathered there. They sat on the platform and looked very relaxed despite the fact that the police picket was not far, in the Bhagatpur haat. The villagers gathered around near the banyan tree listened to the Maoists spell out their plan of action.

When darkness fell, the villagers – both men and women – left the village stealthily. They went one by one, without forming a crowd, under the leadership of a lone Maoist whose name they did not know. They walked with him for almost two hours till they reached a hillock. In front of them was a well-lit highway. At that point, they had no idea what they were supposed to do because their leader had left without further instructions. They waited in the wilderness.

At around midnight, the team leader returned, gathered them together and asked them to follow him. They moved towards the highway; clearly visible because of the headlights of passing vehicles. There they saw that many other villagers from other villages also waited by the road. They waited with them for the signal from their team leader to attack.

Suddenly, they saw an explosion of light. The next moment they were engulfed in complete darkness.

Then they heard gunfire. The Maoist armed guards, who were hiding by the road, started to fire and take cover. The gunfire was coming from the roadside. The villagers panicked and asked the team leader what to do. The firing continued. They heard someone in a ditch crying for help and water. The movement of vehicles on the highway had stopped. After a few minutes, the members of the armed squad came running towards them. They told the villagers to rush back towards the hillock. They ran back along with the other villagers and stopped only when they reached the hillock. There they crouched and waited for the others. After a long time the team leader came and announced that the police had foiled their attempt to loot the rice mill, that many members of the armed squad had died, and that the villagers should return to their respective villages immediately.

That was the only time when the villagers of Tesri came back empty-handed from the Maoists' looting operations. They resolved then and there that they would not involve themselves in such ventures again.

⌘

The Maoists suffered huge casualties that night. They were able to assess the full extent of these only after returning to the hillock, to the site of their planned retreat.

They had been taken unaware by the onslaught of bullets as they had neared the rice mill. It had taken them some time to realize that the police were firing from inside the mill. By the time they had taken cover, many of them had already been injured and immobilized. They didn't know how many were killed at the site because they could carry only a few injured comrades back, under the cover of darkness. When they reached the point of retreat they did a head-count and thanked their stars that they had not kept the villagers at the vanguard. Otherwise, they would have suffered a larger number of deaths and incurred the wrath of the villagers who were their support base.

They gathered near the hillock – their armed guard on alert to counter-attack in case the police accosted them again – and waited for more than an hour, hoping that any of their comrades left behind would join them. One of their experts in jungle warfare hooted like an owl a couple of times to attract the attention of any comrades left behind. But even after an hour, nobody came.

Then did another head-count. It was then that they realized that two comrades, Pawan and Surat, had not returned. Of the four comrades they had brought back from the line of fire, three were dead – Comrade Chander Passi, Comrade Sohan and Comrade Sudama. Only Comrade Shankar was still alive since the bullet had gone through his thigh without touching the bone. In a futile attempt to stanch the bleeding, someone had tied a piece of cloth around the wound. They decided to take the bodies of their slain comrades to Mukhdoompur for cremation.

There was total darkness around. The national highway, about half a mile away, was once again visible because the vehicles had resumed plying. They collected some bamboo sticks from the jungle and fashioned stretchers out of them to carry the dead.

On reaching Mukhdoompur, they laid out the bodies of their fallen comrades near the hut where the senior comrades held their meetings. The bodies were draped in the party flag and taken to the banks of the Kareh in a procession. The comrades present put a bunch of leaves and flowers on the bodies, one by one. Then they formed a line and sang a few revolutionary songs. Finally they fired some rounds with their weapons, saluting the martyrs, before they lit the pyres,

As the bodies burned, the comrade who had led the ill-fated mission thought of the two unaccounted-for men. Were they alive or dead? Had the police caught them? If so, had they revealed anything to the police? The comrade worried about the demoralizing effect of last night's botched operation. People's confidence in the Maoists would be lost.

After the cremation, the comrades went back to their hideout to deliberate on each aspect of their failed mission. But before they left, they sent out a search party for Pawan and Shankar who were still missing in action.

36.

It was a bright Tuesday morning. Chedi Paswan sat on the ground in front of his house, reclining against the wall with his legs stretched out before him. After his nightly patrol of the village – beating his staff on the ground intermittently and shouting, 'keep awake', to ward off the thieves – he would always return to the same spot and lie down on the ground, without a mat or a sheet, with just his blue cotton bag under his head, and fall peacefully asleep, as if this was the best that life could afford him. He had relaxed this way for the last thirty-five years, ever since he'd started work as the village chowkidar, replacing his father who had been a chowkidar too.

Now that the Maoists had taken control of the area, however, he had stopped patrolling in the night. Nobody committed burglaries in the village for fear of the Maoists. The police officers had stopped coming from the police station at night to check on him for the same reason. But he still came back to his favourite haunt out of habit and sat here after breakfast and mulled over his past life, which, he believed had been golden.

He knew everything about the Maoists: when they came to the village; where they held their meetings; who had gone underground with them; and who went to loot the rice mill. Even the Maoists and their supporters in the village never bothered hiding anything from him. He knew everything, but he said nothing to the officer of his police station because he knew that the Maoists would kill him if he did. He also knew that the villagers who had gone to loot the rice mill had come back empty-handed, and that the police had opened fire on them. There were stories circulating amongst the villagers that many people had been killed in the police firing.

Chedi had lost all interest in his work because he realized that what was happening in his village was beyond his control. Moreover, his health had deteriorated rapidly during the last year. His asthma had become so acute that one could hear him breathing from a mile away.

Suddenly, he saw Dukhi Ram, the chowkidar of Jamua walking towards him. Why would the chowkidar of Jamua be coming to see him? Dukhi Ram was not in uniform, but he was carrying his staff.

'The Inspector has called you to Dumri chowk,' Dukhi Ram said.

Why was the Inspector asking for him? But, then, the Inspector was entitled to call anyone he wanted.

Once summoned one had no option but to go. Still, he asked, 'Why is he calling me?'

'Some urgent work.'

'I don't know if I will be able to walk all the way to Dumri Chowk.'

'You will. We chowkidars are trained to walk on the orders of a police inspector even if we're dead,' Dukhi Ram said.

When they reached Dumri Chowk at around one in the afternoon they found a police jeep parked in front of Pratap Singh's teashop. Chedi Paswan immediately recognized the vehicle – it was from his police station. The place was crawling with armed constables, some of whom were in Pratap Singh's teashop, and some of whom sat in a truck parked a little distance away.

Catching sight of the inspector sitting on a chair inside the hotel and talking to Pratap Singh, Chedi went to him and saluted in his clumsy way. Then he went outside again and stood in line with half-a-dozen other chowkidars who had also been called in.

'Have all the chowkidars of the area come?' the Inspector asked his junior police officer who was marking the attendance.

'There are eight present here. The chowkidar from Nurpur village could not come since he is almost blind with cataract,' the junior officer said.

'All right. Take them all to the hospital,' the Inspector said and got up from his chair.

The chowkidars were all piled into the truck and taken to the hospital. On his way Chedi Paswan learnt that there were two dead men lying at the district hospital. They had been killed in the police firing on Sunday night. The chowkidars of the whole district had been called in to help identify them.

Chedi Paswan was tired and breathless from the long walk. The smoke from the diesel engine was bothering him. He felt another severe asthma attack coming on. He closed his eyes and prayed for the journey to end.

When he opened his eyes, a long while later, he realized that they were still very far from the district headquarters. His head was now reeling with pain. He tried to shut out all the sounds and closed his eyes again.

Finally when the truck stopped he realized that they had been brought to the main hospital at the district headquarters. He had come here before to escort dead bodies for postmortem. The junior police officer said, 'All of you go inside the mortuary and see if you can identify the two dead bodies lying there.'

Chedi dragged himself inside the morgue, his limping gait exaggerated by his tiredness. He knew exactly where the mortuary was and the moment he entered it, the smell of putrefying bodies mixed with the smell of chloroform triggered a bout of coughing. When he regained his breath he saw the two corpses; their bloodless faces were uncovered and turned to a side. He knew one of them. 'Pawan, son of Ramu Hajjam,' he said in his mind, exactly as the Inspector would expect him to say it, but he could not bring the words to his lips.

Pawan's eyes were half open, as if he was trying to peer at something just out of his view. Chedi Paswan was struck by an unimaginable grief. He crumpled to the floor, coughing uncontrollably. It took him a long time to regain his composure. He got up only when he heard the junior officer shout, 'Get out of the mortuary if you can't identify the bodies.'

Walking slowly up to the junior officer he said, 'One dead body is that of Pawan from Tesri village.'

'Which one?'

'The one covered with a brown sheet.'

'Was he a high-ranking Maoist?'

'I don't know. He left our village two years ago. Nobody in the village really saw him after that,' he said and walked out of the mortuary. His head was reeling. He wanted to breathe fresh air. His felt his job was over but he knew that his work had only just begun. The dead boy would have to be taken home. There were so many things he had to do. He prayed to God that he should not fall sick, but he felt completely winded. All he could think was, 'What will Ramu Hajjam do?'

37.

On Wednesday afternoon at around three-thirty, when Jamuna Das and a group of villagers were sitting under the banyan tree in Tesri, two trucks loaded with policemen drew up at the village. The first to alight from the rear of the truck was Chedi Paswan, gasping and panting for breath. Four gunmen got off immediately after him and took positions at the four corners of the truck, their rifles on the ready.

Then the junior police officer, looking sheepish and holding a diary and a file in his hand, got off the front. Walking around to the rear end of the truck he barked an order to the constables sitting inside. On his direction, four unarmed constables got off the truck, holding a bamboo cot. The constables lifted the cot onto their shoulders and marched towards the platform under the banyan. Chowkidar Chedi Paswan followed a few steps behind as did the junior police officer.

Jamuna Das and the other villagers were scared to see so many policemen in their village. The village boys sitting under the tree looked petrified – given a chance, they would have fled the scene as quickly as their feet could carry them. Jamuna Das controlled his nerve knowing that it was up to him to behave like the leader he had always purported to be. He stood up but didn't know what to say. He had never seen so many policemen at one time.

The policemen set down the cot.

'This is the body of Pawan, son of Ramu Hajjam. Who will receive it?' the police officer said, giving no details.

At first, Jamuna Das did not understand what he was saying. He looked helplessly at Chowkidar Chedi Paswan in a vain attempt to understand the situation. Then he took the chowkidar aside and had a whispered consultation with him. When he came back he looked visibly shaken. He came back near the platform, where the police officer stood, and looked in disbelief at the body lying before him. Finally he gathered the strength to say, 'His father Ramu Hajjam has gone to the haat and will return only in the evening.'

'We cannot wait in this village for so long. Somebody should go and call him here.'

There was an eerie silence. Chowkidar Chedi Paswan now stood behind Jamuna Das, as if wanting to show his solidarity with the villagers. Slowly other people had started to gather around. They stood mutely watching the developments.

'How much time will it take to get Ramu Hajjam here?' the police officer asked Jamuna Das.

'At least an hour on foot.'

'Is there any other person who can receive the body on his behalf?'

Jamuna Das first looked at the chowkidar, then at the people who stood behind him and then towards the crowd that had gathered at a distance. No one came forward to receive the dead body on behalf of Ramu Hajjam. Chowkidar Chedi Paswan knew that the police party wanted to get back to Dumri Chowk during the daytime because they feared that the Maoists might ambush them after dark. He stepped forward. 'I will. In this village, I can take responsibility for anybody.'

The police officer was relieved and promptly took out a form from his diary, the columns of which were already filled. He spread it out on the platform and pulled out his pen but then he remembered that the chowkidar was illiterate and could only mark the form with a thumb-impression. He rubbed the nib of his pen on Chedi's left thumb and guided his hand to the right spot on the paper. 'Press here,' he said.

Then the police officer turned to Jamuna: 'Now give me your thumb.' He smeared ink from his pen on Jamuna Das's thumb and pressed it down on the paper too. Then he folded the paper neatly and put it back in his pocket. He didn't think it necessary to give them a copy.

As he turned to leave the police officer said, 'Pawan was a Maoist and was killed while he was looting a rice mill on Sunday night. If anybody wants details about his postmortem report and case file, he can come to the police station.'

The constabulary climbed back into the truck. The driver reversed it kicking up a cloud of dust. As the truck pulled away a plaintive wail rang out from the crowd that had gathered in the distance.

It was Phulmani. She knew in her heart that the police had brought home the lifeless body of her son. She ran towards the banyan tree to see her son whose face lay uncovered. She stood speechless near his dead body. His eyes were still open, as if trying to see something; the lips parted, as if was trying to gasp for breath; the face yellow, as if every last drop of blood had been squeezed from his body.

Phulmani Devi stood turned to stone, a deep, primeval grief suffused her being. Her screams, as she fell on her son's body from which all organs had been removed during the postmortem, were soundless.

⌘

While the people gathered around Phulmani who lay sobbing uncontrollably on the dead body of her son, Akbar Mian, who had not opened his cycle-repair shop that day, rushed to the haat to inform Ramu Hajjam of the tragic news of his son's death. A few other villagers volunteered to go with him because they felt that Ramu Hajjam would not be able to bear the trauma of the death of his son and would need their consolation.

They practically ran all the way to the haat. Instead of going to Israfil Mian's shop first, as was the norm, they rushed straight to Ramu Hajjam's barber shop under the neem tree. The haat was completely deserted. No other vendors had put out their stalls. Even Israfil Mian's teashop was without customers.

The villagers stopped when they saw Ramu Hajjam lost in thought, sitting cross-legged in front of the small temple that he had made by the neem tree. They ran up to him and stood behind him. The slanting rays of the afternoon sun fell on their face. They waited for Ramu Hajjam to end his meditation. It seemed to Akbar Mian that the wait was endless. At one point of time he thought to intervene and tell him that he had come to bring him home as his only son was dead. But then he waited.

Ramu Hajjam was deep in meditation; he was dreaming:

⌘

He saw a great saint with a halo around his head and a shining face emanating absolute peace and equanimity. The saint was sitting on a high pedestal adorned with beautiful carvings and a group of people sat on the ground, facing the saint. Ramu Hajjam saw himself there too, sitting among them.

The saint was telling the story of a farmer who was pious, gave alms, observed morality and meditated on the transitory nature of everything in this world. This farmer lived with his family in a village. One day, he went to his field along with his son. While he was ploughing his field, his son collected some dead leaves from the field and set them on fire. A snake resting nearby was irritated by the smoke of the fire, which hurt its eyes. Angry, it bit the farmer's son who died immediately. The farmer lifted the body of his son, laid it under a tree and covering it with a chador said: 'Things which are mortal have to die; all existence in the world is transitory.'

And then he continued ploughing his field as before.

After a while one of his neighbours passed through the field. The farmer told him to inform his wife and daughter that they should send a single meal only and that the maid alone should not bring the food, but that everyone should come to the field wearing clean clothes and incense and flowers.

His wife understood that her son had died. But she also didn't grieve as the farmer had taught everyone in his family to meditate on the transitory nature of life. She along with her daughter and maid put on clean clothes, carried the meal for her husband and also brought the incense and flowers her husband had asked for. The farmer had ploughed his field by that time. He ate his meal under the tree sitting next to the dead body of his son. After he finished eating, the family members collected wood from the forest and placed the body of their son on a funeral pyre, offered flowers and incense, and set it aflame. No one cried or grieved as they meditated on the thought of death while the body was being cremated.

The strength of their virtue was so keen that the Lord of heaven felt the heat of the burning of the dead body. He thought someone was calling him on earth. He realized that the intense heat was because of the virtue of the farmer's family that continually meditated on death. He thought he must reward them, fill their house with seven treasures. So he descended from the skies and asked: 'What are you doing that is emanating so much heat'

'I am burning my son's body,' the farmer said.

'Is it your son or some animal or your enemy? You are creating so much heat , it as if you are roasting the body,' the Lord asked.

'No, it is my beloved son,' the farmer said.

'Then why don't you cry?' The Lord asked.

'He is going the way he had to tread. My grief will not make him alive and, moreover, this is the true nature of life,' the farmer replied.

The Lord of heaven asked the same question to his wife, his daughter and even to his maid. All of them spoke of the transitory nature of life and the futility of lamentation. He was happy with their virtue, their mastery over the true nature of life and their self control. He introduced himself to them as the Lord of heaven and rewarded them with seven treasures so that they didn't have to work in the field and told them to keep on following the path that the farmer had preached.

And Ramu Hajjam could not stop himself from asking, 'And who was this virtuous man?'

'Lord Buddha in one of his many births,' the saint said.

In his dream, Ramu Hajjam wondered why he was dreaming like this. Was the saint saying something to him? Had his meditations given him as much equanimity as the farmer in the saint's story has? He wanted to ask the saint the meaning of his life.

But then he saw in his dream that the saint and the people had vanished. He opened his eyes, drenched in sweat, only to realize that all the dreams he had seen since the day Subedar Singh had beat him, had featured the same saint.

⌘

Ramu Hajjam opened his eyes and saw Akbar Mian and the three villagers standing in front of him. He looked calmly at Akbar Mian without asking any questions. His face radiated great serenity and peace.

Akbar Mian could not stop his tears. He tried to wipe them with the hand towel on his shoulder as he said, 'Pawan is dead. The police have brought his body to the village. We have come to take you home.' And he started sobbing loudly, breaking into wails of grief as he held his friend's hands. 'Ramu Bhai, let us go home. Everyone is waiting for you there. It is our bad luck. We are facing such bad days.'

Ramu Hajjam now understood that his dream had foreseen reality. He got up slowly and said, 'Let me put away my shaving equipment and chair and then we will go.'

Akbar Mian was surprised at his friend's composure – the same man who had been so deeply affected by the small incident in the haat was now so serene, even after hearing of the death of his only son. He called to one of the boys who had accompanied them. 'This boy will put your things away. Let us not waste time. Everyone at the village is waiting for us.'

Ramu Hajjam collected his shaving equipment, put it in a plastic bag and handed it over to the boy who had already picked up the chair. As he was leaving he looked back at the neem tree under which he had worked for so many years. His mind went back to the frisky squirrel that had dropped a sprig on his hand while he was shaving Subedar Singh.

He realized that it had not been an accident.

Ramu Hajjam walked straight and tall and felt a cool breeze against his face. He breathed deeply and realized that his breathing was steady.

He thought, this path too was part of the plan.

38.

Pawan's body was placed on the bamboo cot that had been readied the previous evening by the villagers with as much care as if they were dressing his bridal bed. His body was draped in a white sheet, wound so as to leave his face uncovered. Garlands of strung marigold were placed across his chest. A red cloth was spread on the white sheet on which his draped body lay, indicating that he was a Maoist and a martyr who had died fighting for the cause. Small red flags with the party insignia of the Maoist group were placed on the four corners of his funeral bed.

Despite heavy police presence in the Bhagatpur haat, a few Maoists had slipped into Tesri the previous night, wanting to take away Pawan's body and give him a funeral befitting the party tradition. But the villagers had pleaded with them – Pawan's family was already heartbroken, they said. So, the Maoists only asked that they place the dead body on a red cloth and put the party flag on the cot.

Though the procession was long nobody spoke a word; not even the ritual chant of 'Rama naam satya hai'. Pawan's body was carried by four persons and followed by many volunteers, all eager to shoulder the responsibility of carrying him on his last journey.

Ramu Hajjam walked behind them without any show of grief. Since the day he had been beaten up in the haat, he had walked with his head lowered, his eyes fixed on the ground, as if lost in thought. Today he walked erect and looked straight ahead.

The funeral procession took half an hour to reach the banks of the Kareh. It was the month of September and the river was in full spate, so Jamuna Das and Chowkidar Chedi Paswan decided that the cremation would be held at the proper cremation spot – a platform especially built for burning bodies.

A large number of people, including Maoists from neighbouring villages, were already present when the procession reached. They carried no flags or arms but when Pawan was lowered onto the platform, they began to shout: 'Long live martyr Comrade Pawan!' And, 'Down with police atrocities!' After that, they lined up near the funeral pyre and sang a few songs in praise of their slain comrade and his sacrifice.

A posse of police watched the proceedings from a distance.

The villagers put the dead boy on the pyre and then covered him with a heap of wood. Through all this, Ramu Hajjam stood unmoved. His eyes were without tears, his face expressionless.

When the pyre was ready to be lit, Jamuna Das Mukhia, tears rolling down from his eyes, looked at Ramu Hajjam. 'It is time to set the funeral pyre on fire. What bad luck it is to have to burn one's only son,' he said and broke into a muffled sob.

Chedi Paswan, standing next to Ramu Hajjam, could not stop his tears. Lakhan Singh Subedar gently caught hold of Ramu Hajjam's hand and led him to the pyre. With his help, Ramu Hajjam set the pyre on fire and, within moments, the funeral pyre lit up, burning first the wood and then Pawan's body. The dry wood crackled and the flames leapt up causing the people standing around to take a few steps back. They all stood watching the fire burn. No one moved save those stoking the fire. Except for the roar of the fire and the harsh, raucous cries of the greedy crows of the cremation ground, there was an eerie silence.

Ramu Hajjam watched the body of his son go up in flames without any thought. His dreams could no longer haunt him in traumatic situations. His dreams had no power over him now, as everything he had once feared might happen, was happening in front of him.

It took two hours for the body to burn completely. The Maoists and the people from the neighbouring villages had left once the pyre was lit. The people from Tesri also left by and by, leaving only a few elders and a couple of youths behind. After the fire cooled, they collected Pawan's remains and threw them in the Kareh. Then they all left for their village, tired and emotionally drained. They had nothing left to say, nothing to talk about.

That was when Ramu Hajjam became aware that he had no pain in his heart even though he had loved his son immensely.

He had no remorse or regrets about the life his son had led, and no fear about his own.

He felt as though he was totally free, liberated from fear; that he was finally on a path where everything was vividly clear to him.

39.

After the mandatory death ceremonies that he had to perform for his son, Ramu Hajjam did not stay home. On the tenth day after the cremation he shaved off his beard and moustache, which had grown long over the past two years, giving him the look of a yogi, and left his house to open his shop at the haat that same morning.

It was a very windy day. Dust blew all over the bazaar grounds. Ramu Hajjam went straight to Israfil Mian's teashop to collect his equipment and his barber-chair. Israfil Mian was standing inside his shop and was helping his errand-boy light the hearth. He was surprised to see Ramu Hajjam at the haat so soon after the cremation. He had expected Ramu Hajjam to be utterly devastated.

'You look different without your long hair and beard,' he remarked.

'Looks change with the times,' Ramu Hajjam said. 'And it is best to accept the times as quickly as possible.

Ramu Hajjam collected his things and set off towards the neem tree. When he reached there, he saw Akbar Mian struggling to weigh down the corners of a plastic sheet, which he had spread out on the ground to lay out the tools of his cycle-repair business, with bits of broken brick. A strong wind kept tugging at the sheet, upturning the edges. He was so involved in his task that he didn't see Ramu Hajjam standing under the tree looking intently at him.

When he finally looked up and saw his old friend, Akbar Mian could not hide his happiness.

He got up and folded him in a tight embrace. 'Ram-ram, Ramu Bhaiya! It is wonderful to see you here after so many days. And you are looking so good and clean without your long hair and beard.'

'Poor people like us cannot afford to mourn too long – even for our near and dear ones,' Ramu Hajjam replied. He took his shaving equipment out of his plastic bag, set down the chair to face the neem tree and hung the mirror on the nail embedded in its trunk.

Akbar Mian looked at the area under the tree. The wind had blown it full of dried leaves. 'Let me clean it,' he offered. He took out a broom from his tin box and swept the ground.

After cleaning the area and laying out their shops both of them sat down near the small temple that Ramu Hajjam had built.

After he had been beaten up by Subedar Singh, Ramu had sat in front of the small idol of Hanuman he had enshrined there each day before opening shop. He would sit in front of the figurine and pray for hours.

During the day too, when he had no customer to attend to, he would sit with his eyes closed deep in meditation.

'How come you aren't sitting for prayers today?' Akbar Mian asked.

'There is no need to sit for prayers now.'

'Have you stopped believing in God after the loss of your son?' Akbar Mian asked.

Ramu looked at the small terracotta idol of Lord Hanuman. Regular offerings of vermilion at its feet had stained the floor around the temple orange. He did not know how to respond.

'Now I see God's hand everywhere and therefore I don't need to sit at a particular place to worship him,' he explained.

Akbar Mian didn't understand. He thought that the grief in Ramu Hajjam's heart was making him talk this way. He believed that after a few days he would become normal again. He got up and looked at Ramu Hajjam's stall. He noticed that Ramu Hajjam had not tied the protective plastic sheet over the barber chair.

'You have forgotten to tie the plastic sheet over the chair. Let me do it for you,' he offered.

Ramu Hajjam smiled sadly and said, 'No, Akbar Mian, I don't require a plastic sheet over my chair. These leaves and sprigs, they must fall where they will fall.'

Acknowledgements

My gratitude to:

Shabbir Hassan, for introducing the world of literature to me in my childhood days.

Giridih, where I met *Ramu Hajjam* and felt for him.

Upamanyu Chatterjee, for his support and guidance.

Nandita Aggarwal, my amazing editor without whom this book was not possible.

Sarmad, my son, for his assistance in many ways.

Nuzhat, my wife, for her encouragement to write this book.

Mirza Afsar Baig and Pankaj Jha, for all their help.

The dreams related in the book are taken from the Jatakas, the birth stories of Mahatma Buddha. They have been modified to suit the requirements of the book.

'*Ka Karoon Sajni aaye na Baalam...*' in Chapter 17 is quoted from the 1977 Bollywood film, *Swami*.